Lincolnshire
COUNCIL

This book ~~should be returned on or~~ **before**
~~the last date shown below.~~

Uniformly Hot!
The Few. The Proud. The Sexy as Hell.

THE DAREDEVIL

BY
KIRA SINCLAIR

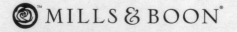

First published in Great Britain 2010
Harlequin Mills & Boon Limited,
Eton House, 18-24 Paradise Road, Richmond, Surrey TW9 1SR

© Kira Bazzel 2009

ISBN: 978 0 263 88131 8

14-0510

Harlequin Mills & Boon policy is to use papers that are natural, renewable
and recyclable products and made from wood grown in sustainable forests.
The logging and manufacturing processes conform to the legal environmental
regulations of the country of origin.

Printed and bound in Spain
by Litografia Rosés S.A., Barcelona

When not working as an office manager for a project management firm or juggling plotlines, **Kira Sinclair** spends her time on a small farm in north Alabama shared with her wonderful husband, two amazing daughters and a menagerie of animals. It's amazing to see how this self-proclaimed city girl has (or has not, depending on who you ask) adapted to country life. Over the past several years Kira has used her Thursday posts at The Writing Playground to vent about the exploits of the donkey, goats, geese and any other animals that wander home with her husband. However, those posts did not prepare her for the joy of seeing her books in print. Kira enjoys hearing from her readers at www.KiraSinclair.com. Or stop by www.writingplayground.blogspot.com and join in the fight to stop the acquisition of an alpaca.

I want to dedicate this book to the men and women serving our country. Thank you for your service, dedication and sacrifice.

Thanks to Lynn Raye Harris and her husband, Mike, who assisted me with my Air Force information. Any mistakes are solely my own.

Lastly, I want to thank my mother and father for their support, guidance and love. They gave me the confidence to believe in myself, the vision to achieve my dreams and a healthy appreciation for the value of hard work. I love you!

1

"HEY, MAGNET, what about her?"

Chase Carden cringed as his friend's voice boomed through the Las Vegas casino bar. Jackson was an excellent pilot, a stand-up guy and a great friend but he had no concept of volume control. Or the fact that while Jackson was loudly trying to scout out a female candidate for the one-night stand Chase's buddies were hell-bent on finding him, Chase was studiously ignoring their efforts.

Not that the redhead halfway across the bar wasn't beautiful or amenable if her stare was anything to go by. But even as her lips twitched up in a seductive smile and her eyes narrowed with appraising interest, Chase just couldn't work up the energy to care.

He wasn't interested. Not in a one-night stand with a woman he'd never met. Six months ago he'd have pushed through the throng of people, leaned down into her space and turned on the charisma that had earned him his call sign in the first place. Lately, it wasn't worth the effort. Sure as hell not three days before leaving for war. There was something about the looming experience that changed your perspective.

Yes, he was proud to go and serve his country. It's what he'd signed up to do. Flying planes was what he excelled at. But knowing there was the possibility he might not come back…

"Why don't *you* go close the deal, Jackhammer? All I want right now is a night out with the boys."

"Shit. Anyone hearing you talk would think you're pussy whooped. I know for a fact you haven't been anywhere near a pussy for months. You need some action boy, before you spend the better part of a year looking at nothing more than sand."

A loud wave of laughter erupted from the twelve guys around him. Part of him could appreciate the joke. Most of him didn't. "Don't make me knock some sense into that thick skull of yours, Jackhammer."

The fact that Jackson was right didn't help any.

"Next round's on Jackson."

Another rousing yell of approval shook the wall behind his back as Jackson threw him a nasty look. Chase just grinned at him. That's what he got for opening his big mouth.

"You having a good time?" Mark leaned across their table and spoke above the noise of raised voices and slot machines filtering into the bar.

"Yeah. Sure." As good a time as possible, he supposed.

"What about that little blonde down at the end of the bar?"

"Not you, too."

Raising his hands, Mark chuckled. "Hey man, no hurt in looking."

"What would Nicole think if she heard you say that?"

The sheepish grin on his face had Chase chuckling too, and looking down the bar.

"Holy shit."

Twelve heads whipped around to stare at Chase, conversations silencing throughout the tables. He hadn't realized he'd spoken aloud, certainly not loud enough to stop his

buddies in their tracks. Clamping his jaw shut, the reverberating shock spiked through his muscles down into his neck.

The one woman he'd never thought to see again, the one
woman who'd dwelled in the back of his mind for the past
six years, was sitting smack-dab at the end of the bar.

Three days before he was scheduled to fly halfway across
the world to Iraq.

"WHAT IS UP with this place tonight?"

Another rousing boom of male voices erupted at Rina
McAllister's back.

"There's a bunch of airmen in tonight."

Rina watched as her longtime friend poured a whiskey for
a guy four seats down the bar. It was nice to finally be in the
same town again. It had been…oh, ten years, way too long,
since they'd lived in the same state let alone the same city.
Despite the years apart, with phone calls, e-mails and spo-
radic visits, they'd managed to maintain a strong bond. She'd
only been here for a few weeks, and they'd already fallen
straight back into their normal, easygoing routine. Sadie was
the sister Rina never had. Hell, she was family. Her only
family, besides the General.

Yelling over the noise, Rina said, "But they usually aren't
this loud." Or rowdy. As the newly appointed public affairs
officer for the Thunderbirds Squadron she was intimately
familiar with airmen. Oh, they could get rowdy with the best
of them, maybe down the street at one of the seedy, hole-in-
the-wall joints you could find off the strip, but not here. Not
at an upscale casino bar like the one Sadie managed.

"Yeah well, several of them are leaving for Iraq in a few
days. I'm cutting them some slack."

Sadie stepped away to fill a drink order. While she waited,
Rina craned her neck against the Saturday night crowd, trying

to see the cluster of men on the other side of the room. The curve of the bar and crush of people blocked her view for the most part, although she could see a few of them on the fringes.

Flyboys. She could smell them a mile away and they tended to group together. Living with one her entire life—her protocol-thumping air force general father—and fending off the cocky come-ons of more men than she cared to count…she knew one when she saw one. And preferred to avoid them.

Fighter pilots were the worst. A special breed of macho daredevils who weren't satisfied with pulling Gs—they wanted to do it with their hair on fire just for show. They all exuded that same mix of swagger and charm, filled with the idiotic idea that they were bulletproof and unbreakable. Rina secretly thought they held special courses during their training—ego-inflating 101.

She supposed they needed that instinctive confidence along with nerves of steel in order to do their job. On the ground though, those qualities tended to rub her the wrong way. She'd spent years worrying about her father and whether or not he'd come back from the latest in a long line of missions. Once he'd reluctantly agreed to ride a desk—his body no longer able to take the torture that came with thumbing his nose at gravity—she'd finally learned to breathe easy again. She wasn't willing to take back that mantle of dread…not for some flyboy.

Sadie slid back to her end of the bar for a few minutes. "Actually, you might remember one of th—"

Just then the solid wall of male moved out of her way and Rina got a great view into the center of the action. And about swallowed her tongue.

"Oh my God. Is that Chase Carden?"

"Yep."

"And why didn't you mention this thirty minutes ago?" Rina fought the urge to reach across the polished wood bar and shake Sadie. "Didn't you think that was something I'd want to know?"

Her disgruntled tone of voice must have registered with her friend. She stopped halfway into pouring a drink and said, "Really, Rina, it's been six years. You guys didn't even sleep together—"

Oh, but she'd been sorely tempted. There was just something about the man that made her brain go haywire, made her body respond, made her lose her hard-won cool, calm and collected outer shell.

They'd met the summer after her graduation from the academy. She'd gone to visit the General while she was on leave. That's where she met Chase. A fighter pilot. The worst possible man for her. At the worst possible time.

She'd known it and yet she hadn't been able to ignore him…or the all-consuming sexual attraction that snapped between them. It was draining to fight against the urges pounding in her brain. Wanting him was a losing battle that thankfully had been interrupted when she'd received her orders to leave immediately.

Fate had stepped in to save her from a colossal mistake.

But even now she remembered the breathless, expectant way he'd made her crave something she couldn't—shouldn't—have. And she'd often wondered what might have happened if she'd stayed.

"I would have thought you'd gotten over him by now."

Rina fought down the warm memory that flushed across her skin. "There was nothing to get over." But there was sure a hell of a lot to remember.

He was laughing. She couldn't hear the sound from this

far away but she remembered the way it had rolled around inside, making her chest tighten.

He looked the same. Several years older but still the same. Dark, dark hair cut a little closer on the sides than she recalled but still long enough on the top to run her fingers through. Even from this far away she could see the stubble covering his cheeks, the dimple in the center of his chin.

A vivid memory exploded in her mind, of running her tongue up from that cleft to the seam of his full lips above. Closing her eyes against an unexpected spike of arousal, Rina turned away. It had been a completely out-of-character—and unwise—action for her at the time. Remembering it now wasn't any smarter.

Forcing the words past the desire clogging her throat, she asked Sadie, "Has he been in before?"

"A few times, I suppose."

"When? How long has he been in town?"

"I don't know. About two years, I guess. He's at Nellis. I guess I thought you would have known."

Sure, like the place wasn't huge. She might also now be stationed at Nellis, but she'd only been there for about a month. She wrote website copy, newspaper articles and press releases—her favorite part of the job. She handled external communications for the Thunderbirds Air Demonstration Squadron, coordinating public relations efforts at each of their show locations throughout the year. She was the point of contact for all media inquiries about the program and keeper of the squadron's public image. She did not study the attendance roster for the entire base.

"Sadie. How are you doing, beautiful?"

She'd been so lost in her own thoughts, Rina hadn't noticed him walking up to the bar.

"I was wondering when you were going to come and say hello."

"You looked a little busy when I first came in."

Two feet away from her. It was the closest Chase Carden had been to her in six years. The immediate physical reaction that blew through her body was familiar and yet somehow different. She was no longer a fresh academy graduate just starting her career and life. She was a woman, successful, intelligent—and apparently sexually deprived for way longer than was safe.

Sadie reached up on tiptoe and wrapped her arms around his neck…his strong, thick, tan neck. He was taller than she remembered. Broader. More muscular.

"You weren't gonna leave without saying goodbye, were you?"

"Not on your life. That's why we're here tonight. I couldn't go away without seeing your beautiful face one more time."

Rina sat in her chair and watched the exchange, remembering similar words he'd spoken to her years ago. Only that time she'd been the one leaving.

The slow-blooming smile and easy laugh made her gut turn with nerves. She wasn't entirely sure whether she wanted him to see her or hoped he'd not even notice her. Their past was complicated…and he'd always had the ability to unsettle her, make her question things about her life and herself that were better just left alone.

"You remember Rina, don't you?"

Sadie walked a couple steps toward her, forcing Chase to follow her down and around the other patrons sitting at the bar.

"Of course I remember Sabrina." The force of his gaze slammed into her chest, making her forget to breathe. "How could I forget?"

Indeed. It was the only damn word her brain would form. Where was her normal quick wit? That unfailing facade of hard-assed competence she was universally known for? At the moment, the only thing she could concentrate on was the unforgiving throb of awareness pulsing at the base of her spine.

"Are you in town to visit Sadie?"

"No. I live here."

"Really?" Chase cocked his head to the side and studied her for several seconds. She fought the urge to squirm under his gaze. He had the ability to make her feel naked and vulnerable without even trying.

She didn't do vulnerable. She'd worked hard over the past six years to build a life and career that she was proud of—that her father could be proud of. She was smart, controlled, independent and she certainly didn't care what this man thought of her…even if the hum in her blood called her a liar.

"Listen, I'd love to catch up with you. Would you like to have a drink?"

No. Yes. "I don't want to interrupt. It looks like you're here with your friends."

Chase's lips turned up in a self-deprecating smile, glancing over his shoulder at the group of men behind them. "They'll get over it. Besides, the chance to spend time with a beautiful woman is more important."

Rina had no idea where the word came from. The last thing she wanted to do was resurrect any part of the past with this man. But somehow "Sure" came out instead of *No thanks*.

SEVERAL HOURS and a few drinks later, Rina found herself walking down the strip next to Chase. They'd stopped at a couple of places. Played a few hands of blackjack.

She wasn't drunk. Really. She never, ever allowed herself to drink too much. She was just pleasantly…pleasant.

If anything, she was intoxicated by the heat of Chase, the way her body tingled from the mere touch of his palm to her back as they strolled down the strip. She was drunk on the power of knowing he was as attracted to her now as he had been six years ago.

It had been that way from the start. Their connection. His effortless effect on her body and the automatic override he had on her brain. With Chase, she felt, acted, was a different person.

Oh, she knew—like she'd known six years ago—that nothing substantial could come of the sizzle between them. She wouldn't risk that kind of attachment…not with Chase. Not now. Not when he was leaving for risk and death and macho feats of heroism.

But she could have this one night. This one chance to slake the physical ache thrumming low in the center of her body. In a few days he'd be gone and she'd never see him again.

The normal Rina, the perfect Rina, the live-by-the-code-of-military-conduct Rina wouldn't approve. But she'd gotten lost somewhere tonight and the adventurous Rina wanted to feel the slide of Chase's skin against her own.

He looked down at her with heat-glazed eyes full of appreciation and the center of her stomach seemed to disappear. She had to look away. Either that or go up in flames in the middle of the Las Vegas sidewalk.

A bright display of flashing colors caught Rina's attention. Blinking neon wasn't unusual, not on the strip, but the words in shiny pink were.

Fake Vegas Weddings
Punk Your Friends and Family

"Oh my God! How funny."
Tugging on his elbow, she headed straight for the sign,

pulling him behind her. It was attached to a strip of shops. One of them was a tacky, touristy place where you could dress in a costume and have your picture taken. It was attached to a low-rent version of the obligatory Las Vegas wedding chapel.

It was something she'd seen a thousand times. But this place was hocking a different angle. This place was for all the people who went on vacation with the ring of their family's and friends' warnings in their ears: *Don't you dare come back married.*

Through the window she could see an array of costumes— Southern belle hoop skirts, Confederate solider uniforms, pirate outfits, kilts. Throughout the room there were several sets to correspond with the outfits—an old-timey portrait backdrop, the bow of a ship, the jagged edge of highland mountains.

And an arched white trellis covered with roses and a sign that read, Elvis Available Upon Request.

"That's so tacky." She swirled around to face him, a huge smile on her face.

"What? You don't want Elvis at your wedding?"

Rina scoffed. "I don't think so."

Turning back, her hands splayed across the glass as she leaned in for a closer look. Chase bunched up behind her. She could feel the heat of him at her back, soaking through the satisfying haze of wine and her light cotton sweater.

"Let's do it." His words rumbled low against her ear.

"Do what?" She knew exactly what she *wanted* to do with him.

"The Elvis wedding."

"What?" That wasn't what she'd had in mind.

"Come on. Marry the soldier before he goes to war." Chase leaned down over her body as she watched his reflection in the glass. His bigger-than-life smile. That mischievous twinkle in his eyes. He was so different than she was. So…daring.

She shouldn't.

His arms tightened around her waist, dragging their bodies closer together. Rina fought the urge to let herself lean against him, the desire to have him kiss along the nape of her neck. Tonight she'd left her hair uncharacteristically down. She always seemed to be in uniform, but the upswept, severe style required by the air force did have its advantages. Unconsciously, she dipped her head to the side, making her hair fall away.

His breath caressed her exposed skin as his fingers brushed against the outside curve of her arm, sending a shudder down her spine.

"It might be fun." Her words sounded fast and shallow. Right now she'd agree to anything, if only he'd move closer.

"Just promise me you won't send the pictures to the General. I do not want to be responsible for his heart attack."

She laughed as his reflection in the window pulled a grimace. She could understand. It probably wouldn't be good for his career to piss off a major general, even if he was stationed half the country away at Tyndall.

"I promise."

Chase backed away, and Rina ducked under his arm as he held open the door for her. A bell rang out through the space. Within a minute a woman materialized from the back.

"Can I help you?"

Chase answered, "We'd like the wedding package please, complete with Elvis."

God, what was she doing? The thought of a wedding—even a joke wedding—was sending her heart rate skittering a little too fast.

Most girls grew up with the fantasy of their wedding in their heads—white dresses, fragrant flowers, flickering candles.

Not her. She'd grown up with the memories of her parents screaming, the experience of her mother's funeral, the idea that two people could make each other so miserable they self-destructed…and took their child's sense of security with them.

"Just fill out these forms for me. Feel free to pick out a gown and tux from over there when you're done."

The woman placed several pieces of paper before them. Rina stared down at the tiny boxes. The little lines wavered for a moment before straightening out again.

Chase shifted closer, planting one foot between her own spread feet. The heat from his body fractured the thoughts racing through her head. He felt so good against her.

What was she thinking about? Oh, the wedding. But it was just a joke. Nothing more. Besides. She was being reckless, fearless Rina for once.

Looking down, she started to fill out the paperwork.

"Constance. I didn't realize your middle name was Constance." His chest brushed against the curve of her back, his hand snaking around the circle of her waist to hold her flat against him. Her throat went tight at the sensation.

"That's because I don't like it. My father picked it. It was my aunt's name." Her words were forced, breathy. She sounded like someone else, some seductive siren—someone she'd never been or could be.

"You're right. I like Sabrina much better."

"I don't like Sabrina either…it was my mother's middle name. No one calls me Sabrina." Not since her mother had left when she was five. That's when the General had begun to call her Rina.

He stared down at her with a heat that had her knees melting out from under her. "Maybe someone should."

Thank God for the counter.

Maybe she should take a step back before she jumped him right on top of the glass. That was taking reckless too far.

"Done." Smacking her pen on top of the papers, Rina turned and headed for the dresses hanging on the far wall. She needed to get away from him for a minute, to breathe some air that wasn't permeated with Chase. What was wrong with her? She wasn't the sort of woman to contemplate grabbing a man and devouring him in public.

Whipping through the rack, she picked the first one that was her size, headed for the dressing room and pulled it on.

Despite contorting herself into a pretzel, she could not get the zipper up. Yelling out, "Can you zip me," she headed into the small room between the dressing areas, holding the strapless number to her chest.

Chase walked out of the other side, dressed to kill from head to toe. The tux he wore might not have been designed specifically for him, but it came pretty damn close to fitting perfectly. Uniforms were great and all, but Rina had a thing for a man in a tux. For this man in a tux.

Presenting her back to him, she held her breath, hoping to slow the rhythm of her roaring heart. He just stood there for several moments. She could feel the weight of his gaze on her back, traveling the length of her naked spine. Goose bumps ghosted up her skin. Beneath her shielding arm her nipples tightened and swelled.

The soft tread of his feet on worn linoleum should have been a warning, but when his fingers touched the small of her back she jumped anyway. She gulped in a large lungful of air, too much, because it rushed straight to her head, making the room waver. A single finger trailed a featherlight line across the indentation at the base of her spine. It took her a minute to realize what he was doing, her brain having malfunctioned at the spike of electricity from his touch.

"Somehow I didn't take you for the fairy type."

Rina turned her head, knowing she couldn't see the tiny picture tattooed on her lower back but trying anyway. Most of the time she forgot it was even there.

"Bout of rebellion the year I graduated high school. It is a little fanciful for me, which is probably why I got it in the first place."

Chase took another step closer, the heat of his body warming her skin.

"Oh, I don't know. You have a whimsical side. I've seen it." His fingers trailed slowly up the curve of her spine. She felt the sting and sizzle at the apex of her thighs as his knuckles scraped over each bump and valley.

"How many men have you let see—" his fingers moved down again, lightly brushing across the picture on her skin before dipping down into the still-open dress to brush the upper swell of her bottom "—that side of yourself?"

Rina drew in a deep, ragged breath before answering, "Enough."

The woman bustled in. "Elvis is here, if you're…I'm sorry."

"No. It's fine. Just let me get this zipper."

Chase zipped her up before moving away. She wasn't sure if it was relief or regret that washed through her. Probably a combination of both.

2

FOR A JOKE, their Elvis was seriously into his role. He didn't break character once as the photographer posed them for several shots. In fact, he even insisted on reciting the marriage vows. Both Chase and Sabrina tried to explain it wasn't necessary but the man didn't pay attention. Finally, they just shrugged and played along.

The whole thing was over in ten minutes. Sabrina giggled; it was a sound he hadn't expected. It clashed with the polished exterior she showed the world. But after seeing the fanciful fairy on her back…maybe that carefree sound was more her than he'd ever realized. He'd always pictured her as studious, serious.

But he'd instinctively known there was something beneath, something she wouldn't let out…something she didn't let free. He'd wanted so badly to rumple her up, to ruffle her calm facade. To leave her mouth swollen from kisses and her eyes bleary with desire just to prove to them both that the passion was there, waiting.

He'd given in to the urge once. And it had been much more than he'd expected. Six years ago she'd taken things slowly— fighting the connection they both knew existed between them. And then she'd been gone.

If the way she flirted, touched and looked at him tonight with those smoldering green eyes was anything to go by, Sabrina

McAllister had changed. And she wasn't fighting anything now. Pure animal lust shot straight to his groin at the thought.

Elvis said, "You may kiss the bride, baby." And Chase found himself indulging in a fantasy six years in the making—kissing Sabrina McAllister. The sensation was somewhere close to pulling a Split-S.

The woman behind the counter handed them an envelope with several photographs. Chase paid for them—the damn things cost two hundred dollars. He hadn't realized a joke could be so expensive. Although, he'd have paid a hell of a lot more than that for a chance to kiss her again.

They walked back out into the night together as she looked at the pictures. They were hilarious. And she was beautiful. Sabrina laughed at the expression on Elvis's face, flipping through them quickly. Until she reached the last one, the one of their kiss, and she seemed to still.

The photographer was good. He'd captured every last speck of desire that had coursed through Chase's lips and into Sabrina. Her body arched into the strength of his hold. Her fingers dug into the shoulders of his tux, drawing him closer. Just looking at the image fired his blood all over again.

Rina stopped in the middle of the sidewalk, pulling him still beside her. The city bustled around them. Even at this late hour no one was ready to let the night go. He certainly wasn't.

Neither was she. Turning to face him, she said, "Kiss me again."

He didn't need a second invitation. Wrapping his arms around her, Chase pulled their bodies close. The world moved on without them. People passed by, talking. Neon lights blinked on and off. And a blast of noise from a nightclub down the street burst into the silence that had surrounded them.

But nothing mattered. Nothing except the feel of Sabrina against him. The heat of her lips beneath his. The heady scent of her, more intoxicating than the alcohol he'd drunk hours before.

Her hands grabbed onto the nape of his neck and tugged, tugged harder, needing more.

He obliged, opening his mouth wider, taking her in.

After several moments Sabrina pulled back, staring up at him with passion-filled eyes. Her chest rose and fell against his own with each ragged breath. His arms tightened, wanting to hold her closer. Feel her closer.

"Do you want to come back to my place?"

Her words whispered against his skin, coaxing him to make the quick, easy decision. But there was nothing easy about Sabrina. And there had certainly never been anything easy about their…attraction. And the fact that he would be leaving in less than three days made this much more complicated than it should have been.

Why could they never seem to get it right?

"No."

Her body stiffened and she tried to pull away. Chase kept a tight hold on her, not willing to let her go a second time.

"Since we're playing at weddings I think maybe we should do it right. Wait here for me."

Walking into the MGM Grand, the nearest hotel, Chase quickly registered for a room, arranged for a bottle of champagne and a small white wedding cake to be delivered and then returned for Sabrina.

He half expected her to be gone. But she wasn't. In fact, he didn't think she'd moved an inch from where he'd left her.

Grabbing her, he placed a quick kiss to her lips but ended it before they could get sucked back into the jet wash of desire.

"Come on."

Chase watched her as she walked through the darkened, gilt-edged lobby heading for the elevator doors. The sway of her hips, the fall of her hair across her back. The way she glanced furtively behind her, those green-and-gold-shot eyes full of sensual mischief.

His body was taut, his hands curled into hard fists to keep from reaching for her in the middle of the packed lobby.

They stepped onto the elevator with a handful of other guests, far too crowded for his happiness. If they'd been alone…

His eyes roamed down the length of Sabrina's body. His muscles tightened at the thought that in a few minutes she'd be his…after six long years of waiting.

His eyes met hers in the reflection of the polished gold doors; it was wavy and imperfect but he could still see the flare of awareness in the eyes that watched him back. Her skin flushed a delicate pink and her breasts lifted on an intake of breath.

A chime jolted him, the doors slid silently open and Chase realized they'd finally reached their floor. With a hushed sigh of thanks, he swooped in to grasp her waist and carried her along with him into the deserted hallway.

He couldn't keep himself from touching her any longer. His mouth found the edge of her jaw and nibbled. His hands tightened on her hips, pulling her back into the cradle of his body. And the scent of her, innocent and yet somehow heady, took over his senses.

He opened their door, Sabrina eagerly pushing against it to get inside. The bed was twenty steps away but it might as well have been a football field. He'd waited long enough for her and he couldn't wait anymore.

Grabbing her by the waist, he pressed her back against the nearest wall, kicked the door shut behind them and sank his teeth into the curve of her neck. She whimpered but didn't draw away. Instead, she arched higher, silently asking for more.

Sabrina tore at his clothes, popping buttons and ripping at zippers. She was just as mindless and eager as he was. And that realization sent him over the edge of control.

Tearing at the shoulders of her sweater, he relished the give of material as fastenings gave way and the cotton fell to the edges of her elbows.

Her nails raked down the wall of his chest, sending his muscles dancing with pleasure. One of her legs wrapped around his hip as he trailed his mouth down the center of her body. She was soft and silky, feminine and perfect, a sharp contrast to the wild, burning urges coursing through his blood. He latched onto one erect nipple through the dark blue satin of her bra. He wanted to take it off, to feel her skin against his tongue and lips. But that would have required letting her go.

For now he contented himself with forcing the hem of her skirt up around her waist and finding the heat of her sex, hot, wet and swollen for him.

He groaned, a tortured sound in the back of his throat that died as her hand wrapped tight around his aching cock.

She squeezed and stroked, splintering his thoughts into mindless, numbing pieces. Her head rolled back against the wall as she arched into his own penetrating touches.

Her eyes glittered at him, jagged and deep, an earthy green. Knowledge and possession. She knew exactly what she was doing to his body as her fingers teased his rigid flesh. She pulled a condom from somewhere, ripped open the package and rolled it with agonizing slowness down his throbbing cock.

She was a witch. There was no denying it. He'd never been this hard, this delirious, this lost in his life.

But he had power of his own, a confidence that he could bring her to her knees with a single-minded assault on her senses. He'd seen her reaction to him, the way her eyes had watched him in the reflection of that elevator. He knew they'd had a connection six years ago…and it had only gotten stronger.

His thumb rolled against her clit as his fingers worked the sweet spot hidden inside her body. Her breath caught in her throat, finally releasing in a stuttered moan.

Her fist tightened around him and her caresses increased to a delirious rhythm.

"Not yet. Not yet." He wanted this moment to last longer. He'd waited too long for it to be over in a frenzied rush.

"No. Now, Chase. Now."

Her panted plea was his undoing. Without another thought, he thrust inside her, relishing the tight, wet feel of sliding home.

Her body tensed for half a breath before going liquid in his arms. She wrapped her ankles around his back, locking them both in place. Her heels dug into his thighs spurring him on to a quicker pace.

Her hips rocked against him, in perfect tune with his own rhythm and needs. Faster, stronger, harder, they both rode until finally he felt her inner walls begin to pulse and contract around him. A jagged cry fell from her parted lips.

That small miracle was all he needed to send him over the edge, the world graying to black on the guttural sound of his own release.

It was several minutes before he realized that his eyes were closed, before his body could draw in enough oxygen that his brain began to fire again. Opening his eyes, he looked down into Sabrina's green gaze.

"That was sure as hell worth waiting for."

The sound bubbled up from somewhere deep inside her. Laughter burst out with the same abandon he'd witnessed moments before. His chest tightened at the sound. He liked it.

Gathering her into his arms, he carried her over to the bed and carefully placed her in the center before slipping into the bathroom.

She was right where he'd left her when he returned a minute later. He couldn't help but stare down at her. She looked amazing, honey-blond hair falling down around her face in a riot of curls. She usually kept it ruthlessly under control. Just like everything else in her life. At least she always had before. He supposed he really didn't know her anymore…if he ever had. But somehow, she seemed different. Free. Happier than she had six years before.

She was absolutely lethal to his sanity this way.

Her clothes were a mess, half on and half off. It didn't matter. Her eyes glowed with knowledge, sensuality, power. Her skin was still pink from his mouth and hands, and her lips curved ever so slightly into a knowing smile.

"What's that?" She pointed across the room to a table in the corner. Turning, he spied the bottle of champagne and single tier of cake covered in delicate white frosting.

"Every wedding needs champagne and cake."

Shedding the rest of his clothes, he walked across the room and poured them both a glass. Picking up the bottle, the cake and both champagne flutes, he headed back to her. Chase handed her a drink, clinking his own to hers. "To life."

With an impish grin she countered, "To Elvis."

In retaliation he let the cold bottle in his hand slip just far enough that the bottom rim connected with the upper swell of her breast. She drew a hiss through clenched teeth but didn't move away from the contact.

Setting everything onto the dresser, he reached for her, removing what was left of her clothes before picking the bottle back up.

He started at her neck, pressing the cold glass there, rolling it against her nape for nothing more than the sheer pleasure of her response.

Her nipples were already puckered but as soon as the bottle touched their tips they drew into the tightest buds he'd ever seen. Reaching down, he touched the center with the tip of his tongue, enjoying the feel of her icy skin against his hot mouth.

He couldn't resist the urge to suck her inside, to take the full swell of her breast into his mouth. She arched against him, jostling the chilled bottle into contact with his own skin and drawing a gasp at the sensation.

Pulling back, he tipped the neck above her body and let a stream of the bubbling wine pour onto her skin. The golden liquid rolled down a path between her breasts, a single drop pooling at the dip of her navel.

Letting more rain down, he bent toward it, lapping the drops as they collected. Only soon there was a rush, more than he could handle, a river of champagne that overflowed to trickle down into the curls at the juncture of her thighs.

Sabrina jerked as the first cool drops hit. With glittering eyes, she waited and watched as he trailed his tongue after them. Her thighs parted for him, opening wide so he could lap at the mingling tastes of champagne and her desire.

She reached for him, burying her hands in the strands of his hair. Her hips jerked as he licked at her sex, teasing her clit, playing at the opening of her body.

She pulsed beneath him. He could practically feel the hum of her blood pumping just beneath the surface of her skin. She writhed against him, her grip holding tighter.

Slipping a finger inside her sex, he relished the single whimper of need she let out as her body clenched hard against him.

"Let go."

The simple words sent her into oblivion, the force of her

orgasm sucking him in even deeper. She finally collapsed into a heap on the bed with a groaning sigh that made him smile.

Placing featherlight kisses to her sweat-glazed skin, he worked his way slowly back up her body. Taking his time, allowing her a moment to recover and collect herself, Chase contented himself with soft, exploring touches.

And he was rewarded a few minutes later when she reached for his shoulders and pushed him flat to the bed.

Sabrina was nothing like he'd expected…and yet, somehow, he wasn't surprised at the sexy, passionate woman he'd discovered beneath her smooth surface. He'd known there were depths to her—even six years ago—that she simply didn't show the world. And the fact that she was sharing them with him now…it was unbelievably arousing.

"I think we need some cake to go with the champagne."

His erection was hard and throbbing. The last thing he wanted was a piece of cake. What he wanted was Sabrina, hot, wet and wrapped so tightly around him that he couldn't tell where her body ended and his began.

He opened his mouth to tell her just that, but the words caught in his throat as she swiped her finger through the icing and smeared a large dollop down the length of his cock. It was cool and grainy, slightly rough. The sweet smell of butter cream reached him, mixed with the heady scent of Sabrina's arousal.

She tortured him, using a light touch to cover him completely with the sticky stuff.

The tip of her tongue flicked across her lower lip. He watched and wanted. Staring down at him with gleaming eyes, she brought her finger to her mouth and painstakingly licked it clean.

"Sabrina." He wasn't sure whether the word was a warning or a plea, not that it mattered as long as she touched him.

With an impish half smile, she bent down over his body.

Her hair fell across him, shielding her motions from his view. With a single hand he moved it away, locking his fingers into the silky cloud at the nape of her neck so he could watch her.

Her tongue laved him, lapping at his erection as if it were the best lollipop she'd ever tasted. Testing flicks, deep strokes—by the time the last speck of sugar was gone his control was about to snap with it.

With a rushed, "I'm sorry," he flipped their positions and slammed home inside her. He couldn't wait, hadn't the strength to hold back for her this time. But as his body raced toward orgasm his mind registered the signs of her impending release.

He thrust into her, one, two, three more times before throwing his head back with abandon. His body emptied into hers with a force and completeness he'd never experienced before. It was mind-boggling how utterly consuming his need to possess this woman was.

Collapsing to the bed beside her, Chase rolled them both on their sides, tucked her into the curve of his body and wrapped his arms tight around her. His last thought before sleep stole over him was that he wished he didn't have to leave her. Not now when he'd finally found her again.

LAST NIGHT she had not been herself. And it had felt utterly fantastic.

Rina had spent her entire life being the good girl, the "never do anything wrong" girl, the "never step out on a limb or take a chance or do something fun and spontaneous" girl. Her life was mapped out, every decision carefully made. At least every one before tonight.

She'd worked hard to fast-track her career. To be the best of the best in her field. To eventually achieve her goal of being in the Pentagon public affairs bureau. She'd worked hard to live down deficiencies—hers and her mother's.

But last night…she'd felt amazing and…free.

Now she needed to go.

Chase was leaving in three—no two—days for Iraq anyway. It wasn't like this was going anywhere. It had been fun. And amazing. And the best sexual experience she'd ever had.

But she couldn't stay and watch him pack up and leave.

It was over. And she needed to get out of here.

Quietly gathering her clothes, Rina fought the fierce edge of a blush as her eyes landed on the dresser and the half-demolished wedding cake sitting on top of it.

What had possessed her?

She had no idea but Chase hadn't seemed to mind. In fact, he'd seemed to like every last moment. A thrill shot through her body, a mix of remembered pleasure and awakened knowledge.

Rina ignored it, but she couldn't ignore the urge to take one more look at him, sound asleep and sated in the bed they'd shared. The white sheet draped across his body, revealing the strong curve of his back and the tight indent at his hip. One long, muscled leg stuck out from the covers tangled into a knot around him. One arm was tucked beneath the pillow, bunching it to his cheek. The other was flung over the space she'd occupied just minutes before.

Six years ago she'd have killed for a single night with Chase Carden. It had lived up to every last fantasy she'd created in her mind. Surpassed them all, actually.

But now it was over.

Picking up her purse, she spied the pictures lying beneath. Reaching inside, she drew out the last one, the one of their kiss, and left it there.

In two days Chase would leave for Iraq. And as soon as she walked out that door she would go back to the perfect, ordered life she'd built for herself.

Last night had been a dream. But now it was over.

At least that's what Rina thought. Until one week later when their marriage certificate arrived in the mail.

3

DAMN. He was here. And she was not ready for him.

Not that she ever would have been. If eleven months wasn't long enough, a couple more weeks probably wouldn't have helped.

Rina had no idea what to say to him. Her husband. The word rolled around inside her brain, pinching at the corners. How was she going to tell him?

Her eyes followed Chase as he crossed the room. How had this happened?

Oh, she knew the answer. She'd been blinded by lust and intoxicated by alcohol and hadn't paid attention. Some joke.

Eleven months had given her plenty of time to come to terms with the situation and formulate a plan to fix the problem…

She'd done research, had even begun to fill out the annulment paperwork, but something had stopped her. The memories had stopped her. And the fact that her attorney had advised her that things would go more smoothly with her husband's cooperation.

Her husband, who had no idea they were married. Well, he was back in her life now. Home. In Las Vegas. Part of her squadron. Safe.

No thanks to his stupid heroics that had almost gotten him

killed. Every time she thought of it the center of her chest started to ache.

So she wouldn't think of it. He was here now. She had to figure out how—and when—to tell him he was married.

Somehow, telling him about this disaster in a letter hadn't seemed right. Nor had calling him halfway around the world to drop a bomb of a whole different sort than he was used to. The kind of shock she had to deliver deserved face-to-face time.

Yes, she'd been slightly concerned that her husband might meet another woman in the eleven months he'd been gone but, considering he was in a foreign country fighting a war, Rina had figured that possibility was pretty slim.

She covertly watched as Chase met the other officers. He moved with a familiar, well-oiled grace—precision-timed movements he'd honed with hours in the sky. From a safe distance in the corner she let her eyes wander across his body. It was good to see him…whole.

Not that she'd ever tell him that.

The last year of her life was supposed to have been amazing. She'd landed one of the most coveted assignments in the air force. The competition was fierce for each position within the squadron. It had been the culmination of years of work. Her father had been so proud of her.

She should have been ecstatic. Instead she'd spent the past eleven months living in fear—that Chase would die, that someone would discover their marriage, that her entire world and the career she'd spent her life building would be snatched out from under her.

Their one stupid mistake could cost her everything. If anyone in the air force found out that she and Chase were married—and by Elvis!—and hadn't informed their superior officers, hadn't filed necessary paperwork…they could be accused of fraud, demoted, asked to resign their commissions.

Not to mention she'd look like a complete idiot. That would do wonders for the reputation she'd built as a level-headed, competent officer.

At the very least they'd receive a formal reprimand in their files which would kill any forward momentum their careers had. Being stationed in Timbuktu wasn't her life's dream.

Actually, she wasn't entirely certain what her life's dream was anymore. She simply couldn't shake the sensation that something wasn't right. That something was missing.

And she didn't mean her husband. One night together did not make a relationship long enough to miss. No, the sensation had started long before he'd rematerialized in her life eleven months ago. It had just gotten stronger once he'd walked back out of it again.

Rina sighed silently, not knowing what to do about it. Easier to concentrate on the mess she'd managed to create in one shining, unforgettable, destructive night.

She'd had a plan.

A plan that had been exponentially complicated when Chase had been assigned to the Thunderbirds. It would have been one thing if she'd simply contacted him once he got home, presented him with the annulment paperwork and they took care of the problem with no one the wiser.

But now they had to work together. Not to mention that she was in charge of his medal ceremony. A ceremony she'd just learned the President of the United States was planning to attend.

Chase was taking over the third position, right wing, for the four-man formation within the squadron. In all the years they'd both served in the air force not once had they been stationed together…until now. It was sheer luck—or misfortune depending on how you looked at it—that Chase had become an overnight media sensation by saving the life of a visiting senator and his assistant while in Iraq.

The air force hadn't wanted to miss out on that kind of publicity. The Air Demonstration Squadron was the public face of the air force. Who better to place on the team than someone who would gain media attention no matter where they performed?

"Captain Rina McAllister, let me introduce Major Chase Carden. Rina is our public affairs officer."

His eyes settled on her. She could feel them, not by the weight of their study but by the tingling sensation at the nape of her neck. Her shoulder blades itched to roll the sensation away. A plastic smile, not unfriendly but not quite real, died halfway to formation on her lips as he took her in. Something wicked sparked at the back of his eyes right before he snagged her outstretched hand in his.

She'd meant to be professional, to handle meeting the newest pilot for the Thunderbirds squadron with nothing more than the calm indifference everyone would expect.

Yeah, right.

Her palm began to sweat where it rested against his. Her lungs suddenly felt as if she'd sucked a brick through her partially opened mouth instead of much-needed air. And someplace, deep between her thighs, she began to tremble with a muscle memory she'd tried hard to forget.

"Sabrina."

She cleared the brick from her throat, firmly dislodged her hand from his and said, "No one calls me Sabrina." Hadn't she mentioned that to him before?

"I do."

Some nasty urge she should have fought wanted to wipe

the twinkle in his deep blue eyes away. He set her on edge. She didn't like it. Especially not here. Here where she was perfect, efficient Rina.

"No. You don't."

Their commander looked at them, a puzzled frown puckering his eyebrows. "Do you two know each other? I didn't think you'd been stationed together before."

Chase opened his mouth. She had no idea what he might say and couldn't take a chance. She cut him off before he could do damage they'd both regret.

"We haven't. My father introduced us several years ago. It's been a long time, though. Right after I finished the academy."

She'd spent the past eleven months keeping the biggest mistake of her life a secret until she could make it disappear completely. She wasn't about to let one slip of Chase's tongue ruin everything.

Although she could remember Chase's tongue doing other things… Clamping down hard on the thought, Rina tried to refocus her attention.

With a shrug, the commander walked away toward some of the enlisted waiting to meet the newest members of the squadron. Chase lingered a moment too long before leaning in closely to speak in a low, rumbling voice for her ears only, "I don't remember you objecting to Sabrina when I was buried deep inside you, screaming your name."

A bolt of heat shot straight through her, electrifying every nerve ending on its path to her curling toes. His words were unexpected. That was the only reason her body reacted.

It wasn't because his lips were close enough to her skin that all she'd have to do was simply turn her head and they would connect with the sensitive side of her neck.

Her body was melting. She could feel each deserting cell as it went AWOL against her better judgment.

She'd had a speech prepared, had an idea in her head about what this first meeting of theirs would be like. None of the scenarios she'd run through had involved a complete and total sexual meltdown.

Laughter echoed off the wall down the hallway, dragging her mind back from the brink of insanity. Jerking away from him, Rina pulled her spine straight, yanked her shirt flat and raised completely blank eyes to Chase.

"This isn't the place for that kind of discussion, *Major*. It was one night. A long time ago. And it doesn't matter."

WHAT A COOL LITTLE LIAR she was. It did matter. She might not want it to, but her body remembered every last second of their night together. Her stiff little nipples fighting against her standard-issue shirt proved that.

He sure as hell remembered every last second, in living, vivid, Technicolor detail. He also remembered waking up alone in a big, cold bed.

He had not been happy.

Chase had known she'd be here today. Her presence was the only bright spot in the events that had led up to his appointment to the squadron. Any pilot worth his salt wanted a chance to perform with the best of the best. And he did, too. He just wished his chance hadn't come at the expense of several soldiers.

What he hadn't known was how he'd react to seeing her. He'd expected to be angry, a little upset at the very least. He had not relished having the tables turned on him that morning. He was usually the one to back out gracefully after a one-night stand.

But perhaps that was the problem. For him, it hadn't been a one-night stand. It had been the culmination of six years of wondering what they would have been like together if they'd gotten the chance. And the reality had shot his fantasies out of the sky in a blazing burst of orgasmic proportions.

Apparently, she hadn't felt the same—if her behavior then and now was any indication. Instead of the warm, sexy, unbelievably amazing woman he'd held in his arms, Sabrina McAllister had reverted to the calm, cool exterior she clung wholeheartedly to. The urge to fluster her was strong.

It had bothered him that he'd thought of her—exclusively—for months. No woman had ever held that kind of control over his interest before. Plenty of beautiful, sexy, smart women had been part of his life through the years. But only Sabrina McAllister had stayed there long after she was gone.

Maybe it was being in Iraq, with a shortage of time, energy and availability for sexual conquests. But he doubted it. Something in his gut told him it was Sabrina herself. Which was a problem.

He didn't know what to do with her—or his all-consuming desire to possess her again. He'd only talked to her for five minutes and he could barely concentrate on anything else.

He didn't want a long-term relationship.

He traveled enough being a pilot. He was at the mercy of the air force whims. He had no control over where he went or when he'd be home.

But that made his attraction to Sabrina complicated. If they weren't working together he would have simply indulged in a wild affair for as long as it lasted and then walked away when they were both done. But now walking away wasn't an option.

The problem was he had no idea if he could keep his hands off of her. Or if he even wanted to try.

Shaking his head, he decided he didn't need to solve the problem today. A smile tugged at the corners of his mouth as he watched Sabrina stride away. The straight, knee-length skirt of her uniform played against the backs of her thighs.

Each step stretched the material taut over the curve of her derriere. He'd had firsthand knowledge of the body she preferred to keep covered.

It was one hell of a juicy secret. One he didn't mind keeping all to himself.

Shaking away the memories, Chase focused his attention back to where it belonged…his new assignment.

The past several months of his life hadn't exactly been a picnic—and if that wasn't the understatement of the year he didn't know what was.

As if spending each and every day with the responsibility of protecting fighting men and women hadn't been enough, he'd somehow become a very reluctant war hero. A simple action on his part had gotten him way more attention than he'd ever wanted. What had started out as the mistake of a lifetime, losing a multimillion-dollar plane to ground fire, had turned into the media sensation of the nation.

His job had been simple. Protect the convoy heading into the northern part of the country. And he'd failed. Miserably. He'd been unable to help himself, let alone the men and women he was supposed to protect.

He'd simply been doing his job when he'd found the New York senator and his assistant cowering behind a blazing pile of metal after ejecting from his totaled plane. The fact that the man was being groomed to run in the next presidential election hadn't helped Chase any. Nor had the man's undying and unending praise as he'd granted interviews to every damn news outlet in the country.

People had died. Because of his call they'd diverted a helicopter meant to pick up wounded from another part of the convoy half a mile away. Another chopper had been sent but it hadn't gotten there fast enough for some. Soldiers had died— soldiers who might have made it if they'd gotten medical attention sooner. And that was his fault. The mission hadn't been a success. And he sure as hell didn't deserve a medal. But apparently, he was the only one who saw it that way.

The attention did not sit well.

Wanting something to drive out the ever-present visions of torn bodies, burning hunks of metal and agonizing screams, he found himself following Sabrina, reaching out for her. He grabbed onto her arm, stopping her before she could disappear again. "Have dinner with me."

Chase fought the urge to pull her closer into his space. Something in the tilt of her head told him that would not be wise.

"I don't date pilots."

Unable to stop himself, he moved nearer, pulling in a breath of her. The fresh strawberry scent of some female bath product washed over him. It was sweet and innocent, feminine and pretty. It didn't match the passionate woman of his memories. Somehow it didn't match the polished exterior before him either.

"Who said anything about a date? I believe we have some unfinished business to discuss."

The alarm that widened her eyes surprised him. He hadn't expected that strong a response from her. Maybe he'd assumed the wrong thing when she'd snuck away from him in the middle of the night.

"Wh…what do we have to discuss?"

"Why you disappeared, for one. The picture you left was a nice touch." He moved into her space, letting his fingers brush lightly against the cotton sleeve of her shirt. He couldn't touch her more, even if she'd have let him, without drawing attention. "Did you know I took it with me? To Iraq?"

She shook her head, her eyes swimming with emotions too tangled for him to pull apart and name.

She moved away from him, leaving him with a cold and clammy feeling he wasn't used to and didn't like.

"There are things we need to talk about. Dinner tonight would be fine. After that, it's strictly business, though."

He laughed silently as she spun on her heel and walked away.

Yeah, right. There was nothing *just business* about the energy humming between them. It had been there from the moment he'd met her seven years ago and it wasn't going anywhere just because Sabrina no longer wished it to exist.

She might have run away from him before. But this time she had nowhere to go.

SHE'D GONE HOME, looked in the mirror and decided to leave her uniform on. It was a layer. A wall between the competent, military woman she was and the whimsical, reckless side of her personality that only seemed to break free around Chase.

Did barriers work if the person you were trying to keep out—or rather in—was yourself?

Rina didn't know, but she was damn sure going to try.

She looked across the small bar table at Chase.

He was different. She'd been too preoccupied to notice this afternoon, but now that she had nothing to distract her... There was still plenty of his normal swagger and charm to go around, but underneath there was a sadness she hadn't seen before.

Something made her want to soothe it away. But she couldn't. Not and keep herself whole. If she let Chase Carden in he had the ability to obliterate everything she'd built—her life, her career, everything that mattered.

Looking at him, she knew any woman in this bar—hell, the city—would jump at the chance to be Chase Carden's wife. And a small part of her thought maybe she would, too.

If he had wanted a wife, a relationship. If being a dare-devil hero, an aerial jockey hadn't been the single-minded goal of his life.

If it were real.

But it wasn't.

Besides, if they started anything that remotely resembled a relationship their chances for an annulment would disappear like a puff of smoke. And an annulment was the only way for them to keep this whole thing a secret. And keeping this whole thing a secret was the only way they were both going to prevent the possibility of being court-martialed for fraud.

With the simple act of not reporting their marriage they'd both broken several major air force rules. And the air force tended to frown on that.

Chase had broken more by not completing all the required paperwork for entry into the Thunderbirds. There was no way he could have gotten her consent to the assignment…not when he didn't even know she was his wife. Would the air force consider it fraud if he hadn't known about the marriage? Possibly not. But it wasn't worth the risk for either of them.

A simple, quiet, quick annulment and their marriage never happened. If she could just figure out how to tell him they were married in the first place.

"Would you like a drink?"

"No!"

Chase and their waiter both turned startled eyes to stare at her. Rina dropped her gaze back down to the menu in front of her, concentrating on the words, and tried to ignore the blush she knew was creeping up her face.

She didn't want to let him unsettle her. Unfortunately, he did. No man had ever had the ability to set her on edge with a single look the way Chase Carden seemed to do.

He made her feel things she didn't want to feel. Want things she knew she couldn't have. And question the course of her life that had been set since she was five.

Without even trying. That's probably what upset her the most. He had no idea he knocked her off balance. From the moment he'd walked in today she'd felt a little off center, like a ball spinning five degrees off axis—not enough to see, just enough to feel.

"I'm still paying for the last time I overindulged." She gave a halfhearted smile and ordered a Diet Coke. Taking a deep breath, she let oxygen flood her body, bringing with it a familiar sense of equilibrium.

"Better?"

Maybe he had noticed his effect on her. She wasn't sure that was a good thing.

"Maybe." She let her lips twist into a self-deprecating smile.

This was too much. She was wound tighter than a top, while he was sprawled in his chair, one hand resting comfortably around the ice-cold beer, the other slung over the back.

She should tell him.

"How's the General?"

Rina cocked her head to the side, wondering where this was going, and answered slowly, "Great."

He leaned forward, playing with the curling edge of the beer bottle label, his eyes staring straight and true into her own. Blue, deep, dark and dangerous.

"He still pulling your strings?"

The familiar anger welled up inside. She should be used to it by now, the automatic assumption that she'd gotten something—everything—simply because of who her father was.

She'd had to deal with it when she entered the academy, taking more shit than any of the other cadets just because of who she was. They'd wanted to break her. To have her go crying home to daddy. She wouldn't give them the satisfaction. With each assignment, including the one to the Thunderbirds, she'd heard the whispers behind her back. "Oh, *she's* the General's daughter."

Years of experience had hardened her to the reaction but, for some reason, coming from Chase…it hurt. But why should she expect more from him than everyone else? She could count the things she knew about him on one hand. His middle name was Edward and he could make her body hum with desire faster than should be legal.

"No one pulls my strings, least of all my father."

"I think we both know that isn't truc. If it were we'd have had this conversation about seven years ago."

Why was he baiting her? Why was he doing this? Pushing her chair back from the table, Rina grabbed her purse. "This was a mistake."

"Sabrina."

"Don't call me that." She bit the words out as she stalked from the bar.

His voice followed her from the restaurant, through the ever-present casino and into the falling darkness—or as dark as it could get with megawatt bulbs blaring from every direction.

She ignored him, melting into the crowd of people on the sidewalk, blending in to the ebb and flow around her.

That had not gone well. She walked through the throng for several moments, pushing unseeingly against the people and things in her way. After a couple minutes the anger finally peaked inside her and her steps slowed to something resembling normal. Then came the disappointment at losing control of her temper. She didn't do it often, for not much pushed her to the edge, but Chase seemed to have a knack for stirring her emotions.

Of course, if she was honest with herself she'd admit that she'd used the anger as an escape. She wasn't ready to tell him. Didn't know how to tell him.

"Sabrina." His voice was soft. And close. It touched her moments before his arm wrapped around her waist and pulled her out of the flowing crowd.

One minute she'd been walking down the sidewalk, the next she was pressed against a cool stone building. How had that happened?

"I'm sorry."

The heat of his hand seeped into the skin where it rested at her hip. "No, I," she said, and swallowed hard, trying to tamp down the firestorm building inside her. "I'm touchy when it comes to my career and my father. I'm sorry."

"I've been on edge lately, but that's no excuse for purposely baiting you." A sad smile pulled at the corners of his lips. His bright blue eyes flashed, but she couldn't tell if it was from the lights around them or from some internal source she couldn't understand. It only lasted for a moment before it was gone, and his normal cocky facade replaced the surprisingly unsettled expression.

"If I promise never to mention the General again, will you come back inside with me?"

Chase looked down into her eyes, his body holding her hostage against the unforgiving side of the building. She'd never known anyone else who, with a single look, could convince the people around him that he was all innocence and sincerity—all while hiding pure devilment underneath.

Normally she was immune to macho charisma and oozing flyboy sexuality. But she couldn't seem to remain unaffected by Chase. Her nose wrinkled. No matter how much she wanted to.

His finger slid from the center of her forehead down

between her eyes to the tip of her nose, smoothing the peaks and valleys as he went.

"That's kinda cute. I don't remember that from a year ago."

"I don't remember much reason to frown."

"But you do remember." He leaned closer into her space, his teasing smile fading away, along with the sounds of a city that never slept.

She could only nod, his eyes holding her hostage.

His hand lifted to her face again, only this time his touch was far from playful. The pad of his finger, ridged and rough, brushed the corner of her lips. He smoothed a path from edge to edge across the closed seam of her mouth. In the center he pushed gently against it, the tip of his finger slipping barely inside.

That simple sensation shouldn't have mattered, sure as hell shouldn't have sent her brain into overload. But Rina could feel her body responding in a way she hadn't felt in eleven long months. The center of her sex grew damp and tingled. Her stomach turned over, wanting more. She pressed the tiny tip of her tongue against his finger and lost herself in a groan of pure pleasure.

His eyes darkened as he reached for her, crushing her between the weight of his body and the merciless wall at her back.

She could feel him, every breath, every muscle, every bone, every vibration. Her head dropped back, too heavy to hold up anymore. But she didn't have to. He did it for her, snugging one palm to her nape, the other to the curve of her throat.

His mouth claimed her with a passion she'd convinced herself had been part of a fuzzy dream. It couldn't have been real. The way she'd felt couldn't be real. The woman she'd been with him couldn't be real. Couldn't be her.

Her back arched into him, seeking more, giving him everything he asked for without hesitation or thought. His tongue thrust inside, filling her up before his mouth moved lower.

Her eyes wanted to close, wanted to surrender to anything and everything Chase wanted to give her. But she wouldn't let them, couldn't, although for the life of her she could not remember why. She focused on the skyline above her and he nibbled at the delicate center of her throat.

A light revolved against the darkness, coming and going in a throbbing pulse that was echoed deep at her core.

No. No, this wasn't right.

"Stop." The word popped out of her mouth on a sigh that held not a wisp of conviction. But Chase immediately took a step away, opening a space between them that she desperately needed.

Rina looked up into his face, ruggedly handsome and stamped with an unmistakable hunger she recognized as the twin to the beast roaring inside her.

He wasn't calm. He wasn't collected. And he sure as hell wasn't charming as his chest rose and fell with the same labored pattern as her own. Wild was what she'd have called him, if she'd had brain power enough to think of a label.

"Too fast." The words whispered up from somewhere deep inside her.

"Not fast enough."

"Slow down, cowboy. I have no intention of sleeping with you."

"You may not intend to but you're going to anyway."

Now that was the cocky pilot she knew.

"I don't think so. Unlike men, we women tend to think with our brains instead of our anatomy. I won't deny that I'm still sexually attracted to you, flyboy, but trust me, I can resist."

His eyelids lowered to half-mast, covering glittering

sapphire eyes. His lips turned up at the corners in a mocking imitation of his full-blown smile.

"We'll see about that."

Rina watched as he turned and walked back out to the crowded sidewalk.

She let the wall take the weight of her body from her shaking, saggy knees. Her head hit the veined marble as she realized she'd just made a tactical error with one of America's best aerial dogfighters. A tactical error that could mean the next few weeks of her life were going to be hell.

She'd just issued him a challenge.

4

"How'd it go?"

Rina looked across the tiny table in the back of the casino restaurant at her best friend.

"You really want to know?"

It was late. Later than she normally stayed out on a work night, but she'd needed time to decompress before going home and Sadie was the only person she knew in the city who'd be up and awake. Sadie enjoyed her job as night bar manager on the strip. She was tall enough, blond enough and certainly stacked enough to have a more high-paying job as a showgirl, but that wasn't what she wanted—not that she hadn't been asked by quite a few of the casting directors.

Rina had no idea how they'd become friends. Maybe it was because they were complete opposites in just about every way.

Not that it mattered. The moment she'd met Sadie her sophomore year of high school they'd clicked.

"Yes, I want to know. How did he take the news?"

Rina dropped her head onto crossed arms atop the corner table, the polished wood and cotton eating her muffled words. "I didn't tell him."

"What?"

She lifted her head but only far enough to see her friend over the safety of her arms. "I chickened out."

"Rina." The single word reminded her more of her father than she'd like to admit.

That man knew how to fill one word with more disappointment and censure than anyone she'd ever met. She'd spent her entire life trying to avoid provoking that tone of voice. Trying to be different from her mother, the woman he was constantly telling her she was the spitting image of. The woman who'd deserted them both before managing to kill herself and injure a father and his son while driving drunk.

The woman she never wanted to be. The woman she saw in the mirror every time she looked.

If the General ever found out about this mess, he'd be so disappointed.

He'd run their house like he'd run his men. He'd always held high standards, for himself and everyone around him. Sometimes the pressure to live up to those expectations had been heavy to bear. But she had. Because she was a McAllister.

Not that any of that mattered anymore. What did matter was the mess she'd gotten herself into. Which she had made infinitely worse by letting Chase kiss her. Where was her damn self-control when she needed it?

"You're right. I wouldn't have told him anyway. I was too busy letting him suck the skin off my neck." She let out a groan and dropped her head back onto her arms. She really didn't want to see the look on Sadie's face.

"Sabrina McAllister."

The shock in Sadie's voice was exactly what she'd expected.

"It's about time you had some fun. And I say who better to give you a little sexual satisfaction than your husband?"

"Sure. If I wanted to stay married, which I don't. The minute I sleep with him any hope of an annulment goes out the damn window. Before, we didn't know we were married. Now we do."

"So what if the judge doesn't find out?"

Rina cut her eyes over the top of her arms.

"Have you seen my life lately? He'd find out."

"So what? Then you get a divorce."

"Then the General finds out, along with my commanding officer, and all hell breaks loose. We're breaking about a million regs right now. Frankly, I've spent most of my life avoiding disappointing the General. Somehow, I think causing an air-force-wide scandal would crash that effort."

Sadie rolled her eyes in a familiar gesture that did little to help Rina feel better. "You need to stop worrying about what your father thinks."

"Yeah. Easier said than done."

"No. No it isn't."

Rina sighed. Her friend simply didn't understand. She had no idea how to turn off twenty-nine years of pleasing the man. It was a firmly entrenched habit.

For most of those years they'd only had each other to rely on. She'd watched him dedicate his life to a career that had often taken him away from her for long stretches at a time. His job was dangerous. Even at five she'd realized she could lose the only person in her life, the only parent she had left, at any moment. It had instilled in her a need to make him happy whenever he *had* been there. A need to be different from the woman who'd yelled, complained and made their lives miserable before deserting them both. A need to be dutiful and strong and perfect where her mother had been flighty and vain and selfish.

"What I *need* is to figure out how to tell my husband we're married."

CHASE HEARD the knock on his front door. For about five seconds he entertained the hope that Sabrina would be there on the other side. He knew it was futile but he couldn't seem to stop himself. He hadn't exactly handled things well tonight.

"There was a rumor you were back in town." Nope, not Rina, but someone almost as good.

"Jackhammer." Slapping his best friend on the back, Chase ushered the man into his new apartment. "You want a beer?"

"Hell, no. I'm not going to drink with you. I'm mad as hell at you." Jackson stopped in the middle of Chase's living room, arms crossed over his barrel of a chest, glaring across the space at him.

There was a reason he'd been chosen for the Basic Cadet Training Cadre as a second class during their years at the academy. The man could be damned intimidating.

"Mad? What the hell did I do?"

"You're alive."

"Of course I'm alive."

"There's no 'of course' about it. Almost a year in a combat zone and I didn't hear from you more than two or three times. I had to learn that you were back in town from one of the newbies."

Chase fought down a wave of guilt at that. It was true. He really hadn't kept in touch with anyone back home while he was gone. He hadn't wanted to. What could he tell them? How unbelievably appalling war conditions could be? How he'd made decisions that had cost men and women their lives?

He hadn't written home because there was nothing worth telling.

"Don't take it personally, man. I barely wrote to my mother and sister either."

His mother and sister had e-mailed him on a regular basis

but…it wasn't like they'd exactly been a close-knit group before he'd left for Iraq. His mother and sister had always been close…closer still after his parents' divorce. They'd had a mother-daughter bond he hadn't ever been a part of. Chase had been left with no one when his father disappeared from their lives.

So, no, they weren't close. They were simply family.

"Cut me some slack. I'm not even settled yet. I would have called you in a few days."

"Yeah, right."

Marching into his kitchen, Jackson pulled a beer out of the fridge, plopped down onto the sofa and dropped his feet onto the coffee table—the two lone pieces of furniture in the entire room.

"So, how was it?"

Hell. Chase stared across at the other man. "God, it's good to see you."

"Now you get all mushy. You aren't gonna cry, are you?"

"No." Grabbing a beer of his own, Chase sat down beside his buddy. "Look, I'm sorry. I really didn't think it would matter. I never thought you'd expect weekly reports."

"Yeah, I know." Jackson pulled a face before brushing the subject aside. "It doesn't matter. So, I hear you're a war hero."

"Not really."

"The air force doesn't award the Distinguished Flying Cross for nothing. I'm getting an invitation to the ceremony, right?"

Between coming home, joining the squadron and seeing Sabrina again, he'd almost forgotten about that mess. Or maybe it had been convenient selective memory.

He didn't want the honor. He didn't deserve the damn medal. Somewhere along the way the media had gotten and run with a skewed version of the events of that night that the world seemed to accept at face value. He had no idea where the misinformation had come from…not that it really mattered. People believed what they wanted to believe.

"Sure. The damn President's coming. Why shouldn't you?"

They should all have a huge party. Then maybe he could forget about the truth of what had really happened that night.

DONALD BLANKENSHIP STARED down at the piece of white card paper in his hand. Simple, plain, with stark black lettering and crisp precise words. He'd typed out the envelope, stamped it; now all he had to do was slide the note inside and mail it.

His eyes strayed to the picture sitting beside his desk. The picture of his little girl. Only she wasn't little anymore. Hadn't been for a very long time.

The pigtails and tap shoes had long been replaced by an army dress uniform and ACUs. The young woman stared back, unsmiling, serious. So grown-up.

His Amy had been so excited to join the army. To serve her country just like her father had for twenty-five years in the air force. He'd been so scared to watch her go, not sure when she'd come back.

She had, finally. In a flag-covered box.

It had been easy to risk his own life in service to his country. It had been difficult to watch his only child do the same. And it had been hell when she'd come home in a casket.

His vision wavered. He fought against the weakness of tears. Amy wouldn't want him to cry, to be sad. But he couldn't help it. His world wasn't right without her in it.

His attention landed back on the card in his hand. His daughter might have died serving her country, but her death wasn't the result of enemy fire. No. They hadn't told him his

Amy had died needlessly. He'd learned that on his own. Asking the right people the right questions. She'd been alive on the battlefield. She could have—would have—survived if she'd gotten medical attention.

A soldier—an airman—was responsible for her death. Someone who'd placed their own life and the life of a senator—someone who shouldn't have been in the middle of a damn war zone in the first place—above his daughter's. Above everyone else's.

And now they were giving him a medal.

The man didn't deserve a medal. He deserved to suffer.

Just like he did every day without his Amy.

"HELLO, BEAUTIFUL."

"Chase." Sabrina jerked guiltily at the sound of his voice, surprise widening her eyes behind the magnifying lenses of her glasses. She'd been staring, unseeing, at her computer screen for God only knows how long. "What are you doing here?"

And apparently, from his negligent stance against the side of her open office door, it looked like he'd probably been there long enough to realize she was daydreaming. Luckily, he had no idea her thoughts had centered on the kiss they'd shared last night.

Uncrossing his arms, Chase walked further into her office, circling around to stand behind her chair. He didn't lay a hand on her body. Evidently, that wasn't necessary in order to send a shock of awareness shooting through her. Her muscles pulled tight, as if anticipating a blow...or caress.

His breath brushed against the nape of her neck where she'd pulled the hair up and off as per regulations. For once she wished she could have left the mess down. Her heart sped up. She wanted nothing more than to get away from him before he could do more damage to her resolve.

She swiveled her chair as far out of his atmosphere as she could get without actually getting up. That would be a sign of weakness. She wasn't about to let him know just how much he could affect her without even trying.

Rina eyed Chase over the black rim of her glasses. She only wore them when she planned to be parked in front of her computer for several hours. At the moment, she was thankful for the barrier they put between them.

In one swift motion Chase took that from her, too. With a brush of his thumb up the line of her jaw, he swiped them from her face.

"Much better."

"I hope you didn't come in here to flirt, Chase. I have work to do and this is going nowhere."

Straightening away from her, he folded the earpieces into a neat pretzel and laid the glasses on the corner of her desk.

A half-formed smile played at his lips as he walked away, across her office to the bookshelf she had stowed against a wall. She had no idea why, but that look made her neck twitch and her lip want to curl into a snarl.

"No. Flirting implies fun and games. And I'm not playing with you, Sabrina."

The intensity in his eyes made her breath stutter in her throat. She missed a necessary inhalation of oxygen, and her brain and body both seemed to falter.

There was something unsettling about having his focus centered solely on her. Chase Carden was a strong man. He attacked everything, including his flying, with a single-minded sense of confidence and control.

She suddenly felt a little hunted...and hot.

He smiled at her, a real full smile that actually touched his eyes and the uncomfortable moment was gone. "Vince said you might have some questions for me."

"Oh." She stared at him for several seconds. Somehow she didn't believe the smile. It only made her more concerned.

Turning to her computer, she tapped on a few keys and pulled up the file she'd begun compiling on Chase when she'd been told she would handle the ceremony. It was sad that most everything she knew about her husband had come from the few sketchy paragraphs.

"I have the bio information you supplied with your Thunderbird application, plus some information that was forwarded from your files. I'll print you off a copy of what I have. Feel free to fill in any gaps or make any corrections. We'll be using the information in the program for the ceremony so let me know if there's anything you don't want included."

She pushed a button and the printer at the corner of her desk began to whir.

"I'll also be scheduling a photo session. We need an updated shot for both the Thunderbirds and for the presentation."

They might be in the middle of the off season, but that didn't mean there wasn't work to be done. Several of her staff had taken leave since once they started touring it was almost impossible. The demanding schedule for the squadron was one reason officers were only allowed to serve for two years and were required to have spousal permission paperwork turned in with their application. Serving as the outward face of the air force required sacrifice from everyone, including families.

So, on top of the extra duties involved in coordinating a medal ceremony set to be attended by the President and several high-ranking members of the senate, she had to oversee the new Web site design and write updated copy, organize the logistics of the first several shows on the schedule, contact media outlets for each and prepare press releases.

Writing was her favorite part of the job—Web site copy, press releases, internal squadron newsletters—it didn't matter, putting words to page always gave her a sense of accomplishment. And she was damn good at it. She'd received several Public Affairs Achievement Awards.

"Oh, and I've received a request from the *Review Journal* for an interview. I'm going to grant it. I'll let you know when the appointment's set for. My understanding is they want to interview you there but will be sending out a photographer to get some photos in the next week or so."

The heat was fading from her body but for some unexplained reason she wasn't ready to look at him again. Instead, she picked up the pages from her printer and began reading them.

"'Babe Magnet.' I bet you just loved that."

Call signs were a funny thing. You couldn't name yourself, not without being thought of as a self-righteous prick. The other members of your squadron assigned the moniker to you. You had no say and could give no input. And usually they were insulting or derogatory. She'd seen some doozies over the years.

However, from what she understood, Chase deserved every last syllable.

"Something tells me the immature idiots who gave it to you thought they were doing you a favor."

Chase stood against the far wall of her office, his damnably well-muscled arms crossed in front of his equally drool-worthy chest. It always amazed her how a man who spent most of his days sitting in the cockpit of a plane could have muscles like that. His dark chocolate hair was slicked back from his head. Either he'd just had a workout, shower or more likely both.

"Let's just say that at the time I deserved it." Gone was

the playful hint of mischief he'd carried into her office with him, replaced by a serious intensity that she absolutely didn't understand. "However, the only thing I seem to be attracting lately is sand."

And with a single sentence he could take her from the edge of jealousy—at the thought of all the women he must have slept with to earn the title—to feeling like a heel. While she'd been preoccupied with protecting their secret, he'd been in a war zone. And had almost died.

She needed to tell him.

"There you are, man. Are you coming?" Dennis, one of the solo pilots, walked into her office. "Hey, Rina," he said, and promptly ignored her. That was okay with her. She'd fought hard to become just one of the guys. She had a reputation as a cold, competent member of the team. It was something she'd worked hard to cultivate. Everyone seemed fine with that status quo.

Everyone but Chase. He wanted something from her she couldn't give, not and keep that insulating facade in place. He made her think and feel things she didn't want to think or feel, didn't have the luxury to think and feel right now.

"Yeah. I'll be there in a minute."

Rina expected him to follow Dennis out. Instead, he walked across the room and spun her chair to face him.

He was tall. Of course, most anyone was tall compared to her but from this perspective, she had a stellar view of every damn plane and valley on his body. And she wanted to lick them all. Again.

Clamping her teeth shut against the sudden urge, she fought to regain control of her impulses.

His hands pressed to the back of her black leather chair, tipping her slightly and making her feel ten years old again and about to ride the Scream Machine roller coaster for the first time.

He smiled down at her, his blue eyes flashing fun once again and said, "Next time we'll do more flirting," right before his lips claimed hers in a short, powerful kiss.

She should have kicked him in the balls. If anyone had seen them kissing there would have been hell to pay. Commander Wright was a stickler for the rules—including no public displays of affection in uniform. Instead her body melted and she found herself nodding stupidly.

Damn it!

CHASE STARED down at the piece of paper in his hand.

You don't deserve the
Distinguished Flying Cross

That was all there was. Nothing more.

The words made his blood run cold. Not because of any threat they implied—there really wasn't one—but because they were true.

However, only a handful of people knew that. Actually, only a handful of people knew the factual events of that night. He and whoever had written this card were apparently the only two souls who realized the *truth*. He didn't deserve the medal.

But no one was listening to him. He didn't want the ceremony. Didn't want the hoopla. Certainly hadn't wanted to be interviewed by Matt Lauer and Oprah.

Hell, the President was coming to his ceremony, or at least that's what he'd been told. The air force saw this as a way of capitalizing on some great media attention. And frankly, he couldn't blame them. If it had been anyone else…he'd have told the guy to man up and take one for the team. Which was exactly what he was going to do.

It was one night out of his life in Mess Dress. At least, that's how he was trying to view it.

He slapped the card back down onto the edge of his kitchen counter.

Whoever had sent it, he agreed. Not that he could tell the person. They hadn't even included a return address. He had no idea what they wanted him to do or say.

He strode for the door, leaving the card balanced on the edge of the counter but stopped halfway there.

He'd been headed for Sabrina's house. If there was anyone he'd like to talk to about the whole situation, it would be her. But considering she'd been assigned the task of making sure his medal ceremony and the apparent media circus they expected to surround it went smoothly, there was no way he could do that.

Instead Chase sank down into his dark brown leather chair. It didn't quite feel like his, but it was. It had been in storage for the past year.

It wasn't the same apartment he'd had before but it was in the same complex. His stuff was the same. And yet it didn't seem like home.

Everything here had stayed the same. Only he had changed.

As a pilot he'd had it relatively easy compared to the other guys. It had still been tough, hotter than hell. But he hadn't spent most days dodging bullets and praying a roadside bomb didn't kill him. Air force jets weren't being shot out of the sky on a daily basis. Of course, his would be the exception to the rule.

Being in a war zone changed you. More than he'd expected.

Somehow the extraneous existence that had been perfect for him before now held absolutely no excitement. Eleven months ago he would have been at one of the casinos or bars having a drink, soaking up the pulsing neon party atmosphere.

At the moment he wanted none of that.

He'd lived in Sin City for a while now. Only he no longer had the urge to sin. What he really wanted was to spend the evening teasing Sabrina into a fit for the simple pleasure of watching her anger and passion.

He loved how her green eyes sparked with temper. How her skin glowed warm with conviction. He seemed to be the only one to see beneath her calm, cool surface.

She'd shown him a side of herself no one else apparently knew existed. Sometimes he wondered if she even knew. And now, whenever he looked at her, he didn't see the perfect uniform and pulled-back hair; he saw her lying on that hotel bed, champagne running across her breasts.

Until today, he'd had no idea how important the reaction he could pull from her could be. It gave him a sense of masculine power. A reminder that life went on and he was still alive. A reminder he hadn't realized he'd needed.

Chase's lips turned up into a grin and his fingers played at the arm of his chair.

Sabrina interested him. More than anything in the past eleven months had. More than anything in the last several years had. And whether she wanted to admit it or not she was attracted to him. Hell, they'd already proved how fantastic they could be in bed together.

He could not figure out why she was resisting so hard. She certainly hadn't fought him before he'd left. Not that it mattered. He enjoyed a challenge.

And he could tell Sabrina McAllister was going to be that. But he'd convince her because the payoff in the end…well, that would be better than any G-force induced adrenaline rush. He wanted Sabrina McAllister in his life. More than he'd wanted anything in a very long time. And he had no problem fighting for her.

Hell, high-precision maneuvering was what he excelled at.

5

HE WAS DRIVING her crazy. Everywhere she looked, there he was. If she hadn't known better, Rina would have thought he was stalking her.

But he wasn't. He was just doing his job.

Not that it was helping her much.

How hard could it be to ignore one man? One hot, gorgeous, dark-haired, blue-eyed, sexy-beyond-belief man?

Apparently it was impossible. For her at least.

Which was why she lurked inside the doorway to the hangar waiting for the team to return from practicing maneuvers. She couldn't actually watch the practice. It was the irony of her life…she was deathly afraid to fly.

She'd never had any problems watching the team perform, though, as long as she was firmly on the ground. But for some reason she couldn't stomach watching Chase, just as she'd never been able to watch her father.

The unbelievable scream as they flew overhead penetrated the walls. It scared the hell out of her. Not the sound but knowing he was up there, taking risks each time he rolled into a maneuver or dove for the ground.

The pilots in each four-man formation trusted the others blindly. In order to get such tight and perfect order none of the three following pilots used their instruments. They strictly flew off of their proximity to the lead pilot. That took guts and a blind faith she wasn't sure she'd have.

There had been an incident years ago where all four pilots died in a crash—each following their lead straight into the ground. They'd been doing their job. And Chase would do his, confident in the abilities of the men and women he flew with. Rina didn't have to ask him. She knew that's exactly what he'd say.

It still set her on edge. Even more so after hearing about the heroic and idiotic stunt he'd pulled in Iraq. Yes, some part of her appreciated his selfless act. But another got so fiery mad at him for risking his own life for some stranger. If things hadn't gone well…if he hadn't come back…

It was something she wouldn't let herself dwell on. At least not long enough to get past the complete mess his death would have caused. Trying to explain to everyone that they'd been married would not have been pretty.

Rina wasn't sure she understood the kind of…conviction pilots showed in their abilities and those of the team around them. She didn't think she'd ever felt that way about anything.

Maybe just pilots had the capacity. Her father had certainly felt that way about the air force—still did. She'd thought after the academy she would feel the same way. She didn't.

It wasn't that she didn't enjoy her job, or appreciate and respect the men and women serving with her. Because she did. She just didn't think she had the same level of commitment that Chase and her father had.

But she wanted to feel it.

Rina watched Chase walk into the hangar, flight helmet in hand, hair damp and curling at the edges. His flight suit hugged every damn curve of his body. He looked amazing as he joked and laughed with the other members of the team.

She really didn't like the way he smiled down at Major Tracey Burhop, the number four pilot. Babe Magnet. She fought down the urge to drag him away from the pretty redhead.

What was wrong with her?

This was Burhop's second year with the squadron and she'd never had any problems with the other woman, who happened to be happily married. But apparently that didn't seem to matter to the green-eyed monster living inside her chest.

Of course, Chase's reputation probably wasn't helping that any. Neither was the seemingly unshakable urge to peel that flight suit off of his body inch by slow and sensual inch.

She should leave while they were occupied and before she made a huge mistake that blew their lie straight out of the water. But she couldn't take her eyes off of him long enough to move.

"Sabrina." And then it was too late.

"Don't call me that."

"Did you need something?"

Chase walked straight to her, giving her a smile of her own that made her heart go soft and melty at the edges.

"No. Yes." You. What was wrong with her? "I came to ask you a few questions about the ceremony. Do you have a minute?"

"Sure. Fire away."

"I need to get a list of anyone you'd like invited to the ceremony. Obviously, the President is attending along with several high-ranking government officials and Senator King. All the generals. Local officers. Are your mother and sister flying in?"

She looked up into his eyes and wished she'd thought to bring pen and paper to write with, something to occupy her hands and mind. Of course, that would have required forethought and not just an uncharacteristically wild impulse to find Chase for the simple pleasure of seeing him.

"Yes, they're coming. I have a few friends here I'd like to add to the list." He paused. It was a quick indrawn breath that told her whatever he was about to say next he wasn't entirely happy about. "We lost several good soldiers that night. I was thinking about inviting their families, let the sacrifice that their loved ones made get the attention it deserves."

"I think that's a thoughtful idea, Chase."

She could tell by the pinched pull of skin around his mouth and eyes it wasn't something he liked to think about, remember. She could understand why.

"I'll handle it." She'd do some research and take care of this on her own. She didn't want him dwelling on the negatives of that night any more than he probably already did.

While they'd been talking the group had drifted away, leaving them practically alone. She turned on her heel and headed abruptly for the door.

Chase fell into step beside her. As they reached the door, he snagged it, holding it open for her. "After you."

She didn't do it on purpose, at least she didn't think she did, but as she walked past they touched. Her feet immediately stopped. She hadn't told them to…they just did. Air jerked into her lungs, making a sharp whistling sound she really didn't like.

Chase reached for her. The warmth of his hand settled at the base of her spine, giving her the jolt she needed to get the synapses in her brain firing again.

She shot forward as if he'd branded her instead of simply touched her. "I'll see you around," slipped out of her mouth, breathy as if she'd just run PT.

"Let me know if there's anything else you need." The melted honey in his voice told her he was perfectly aware of the effect he had on her body. And that he wasn't talking about the ceremony. "Anything."

Rina hurried down the hall, away from him and temptation. How could the damn man make her body sizzle and her brain turn to mush with a simple, completely nonsexual touch?

Her teeth ground together, the annoying sound echoing through her brain. Rina fought the urge to turn around, afraid to find him still standing there, that know-it-all smile and those dancing eyes staring back at her.

If she looked and he was laughing at her…she'd probably go ballistic.

But when she turned around, he was gone. And somehow that was worse.

NOTHING HAD HAPPENED.

They hadn't canceled the ceremony. No one was even talking about his note. He knew. He'd asked around.

His Amy might have chosen the army, but only because she'd wanted to be a trauma surgeon and they offered the best opportunities for training and practicc. Otherwise, she'd have gone into the air force, "Like my old man," she'd always said, with that saucy, cheeky grin.

Of course, maybe it was his fault that nothing had happened. He hadn't been specific about what he wanted. Obviously, that would have to change.

SHE'D RUTHLESSLY avoided him for several days. And bought herself some much-needed breathing room. If she couldn't control herself and her impulses when she was around him, she'd simply avoid him. At least that was her thinking. The only problem was that just because she hadn't seen him in person didn't mean he hadn't invaded her thoughts, her nights, her dreams.

But now she had the annulment paperwork ready and it was time to tell him. The question was how and when.

Why was this so difficult for her? Normally she tackled

tricky situations head-on. She'd learned early in life that wishing something weren't true or hard didn't make it go away.

So why was she prolonging the moment that would take Chase out of her life?

Digging the heels of her palms into her eyes, she groaned and pushed the paperwork to the edge of her desk.

She had thirty minutes left in the day. She needed to put all thought of her farce of a marriage out of her mind and concentrate on finishing some actual work. She needed to approve the new Thunderbird Web site design, proof some press release copy and make a few phone calls for the first show in March.

Unfortunately, she managed to bury herself a little too well. Her first sign of trouble was when Chase plopped his tight ass onto the edge of her desk, sliding the annulment papers out of his way without even looking at them.

Her heart hit afterburners and kicked into overtime. Without thinking, she reached across and snatched them out from under his fingers.

"What's that?"

Chase reached to take them back from her. Before he could, she opened a desk drawer, dropped them on top of the neatly labeled files and slammed it shut. The sound of crumpling papers made her grunt in distress.

"Nothing."

With a shrug of his shoulders, he let it go. Rina sighed as she settled back into her chair, keeping a foot tight to the drawer just in case.

And then he reached for her, his finger wrapping around a stray wisp of hair that had escaped to curl about her face, sliding the pads of his thumb and finger down the strand.

She licked her lips, her eyes finding his and remembering the feel of them against her own, the sharp edge of that wall against her back as he'd let her go, hot and wanting.

"Don't touch me," she whispered through suddenly tingling lips.

"Why not? I like touching you." He leaned toward her, his mouth moving closer, his body looming over her. "You like it when I touch you."

She jerked, not because his hands, so close to her skin, stroked her, but because they didn't. She wanted that sensation almost more than her next breath. She shouldn't. She shouldn't want this man to touch her. But whenever they shared the same space it was all she could think of. All she craved.

They were married. It was complicated. He was a pilot. They worked together. And if they lost the opportunity for the annulment then they'd lose the opportunity to keep this mess quiet and personal. And potentially lose their positions on the squadron and any forward momentum for their careers.

Still, she couldn't stop her own eyes from traveling the length of his body. She couldn't help herself, not with him perched so closely, the hard curve of his thigh practically near enough for her to bury her head in his lap. A vision flashed in front of her eyes, the memory of doing just that, licking sweet white frosting from his body…

Blood whooshed in her ears, the sound of it rushing from her brain to her now-throbbing sex. Uncrossing and recrossing her legs, Rina tried in vain to relieve the worst of the ache. Unfortunately, it wasn't going anywhere.

And apparently, neither was Chase. She was about to threaten to call someone to forcibly remove him if she had to when his body slid off the side of her desk. He stood tall, pretty damn even with her father actually. Her eyes moved from one wide shoulder to the other, down his arms…and straight to several papers he held in his hand.

"What's this?"

Damn! She should have been paying more attention to what he was doing instead of ogling his body.

"Nothing, Chase." She reached for the report she'd compiled about that night in Iraq, but he held it out of her range. She'd needed some details for the medal ceremony so she could invite the families he'd requested. But she'd hoped to keep the file away from him if for no other reason than to spare him having to think about it all again.

Just reading the reports from that night…it had made her sweat with delayed fear, her chest aching and her stomach turning sour. She couldn't imagine actually living through the experience.

"Doesn't look like nothing."

Rina stared into his eyes for about half a second before she realized he was mad. His body was strung so tight she thought every muscle might snap. His eyes darkened…the same shade as when he was aroused. Why would she think about that *now?*

"Why didn't you ask me?"

"Because I didn't want to bother you, Chase."

"Seems like a pretty stupid decision. Why not just ask the person who'd been there?"

Idiotic man. No one, not even the General, questioned her ability to do her job. And do it damn well.

"I wanted an outside view of the situation, Chase, since I knew yours was a bit…skewed."

"Skewed? My memory of that night is nowhere close to skewed, Sabrina. I remember every last detail whether I want to or not."

"Yes, and it's common knowledge that you don't believe you deserve this medal."

A growl erupted from the back of his throat. The sound made her take a half step back. She didn't fear that his anger would get the best of him; she knew he had more control than that, but the sound still set her on edge.

"You want to know what happened that night? I'll tell you. I made a choice. A bad decision. One I didn't believe was right even at the time but I did it anyway. I evacuated two men who shouldn't have been in the middle of a war zone, two men who'd come there on a publicity stunt not realizing or caring that their presence put the lives of men and women in danger, to safety. I placed their lives above those of the men and women fighting and dying around us."

He finally looked at her again. Gone was the anger, replaced by a tearing pain and guilt that ripped into her gut. She'd had no idea. She'd known he was upset, with himself and the situation, but she hadn't realized how deep the pain went. How much he tortured and blamed himself. For something he couldn't have controlled.

"You did the right thing, Chasc. The senator and his assistant weren't trained for battle."

"That's what everyone keeps telling me. It doesn't matter. I could have done my job better in the first place and no one would have needed to be rescued."

Without waiting for her to say anything more, he spun on his heel and walked away, leaving her with a huge aching hole in the center of her chest.

How THE HELL do you tell someone they're married?

Rina thought the Band-Aid approach was probably best. She sat in her car, looking up at Chase's apartment. She had to do this tonight. She had to see him. The way he'd left this afternoon…she couldn't leave things that way. She couldn't leave him hurting and alone. Although, she supposed she was about to make the whole situation worse.

At least he'd have something else to concentrate on.

The General would tell her to buck up. To do what she knew was right. How come doing the right thing had never gotten any easier than it had been when she was six and accidentally broke her grandmother's antique vase?

Somehow she didn't think this could be fixed with some super glue.

If the only thing she had to be worried about was his reaction to her news…then she wouldn't be so uptight.

The real problem was that she didn't trust herself. Not around Chase. The more she saw him, the more he touched her, teased her, tempted her, the more she lost the will to resist. She wanted him more each and every damn day until she wasn't certain she'd be able to control the urge the next time they were together.

She didn't like feeling that out of control of her own actions.

For almost a year she'd chalked her stupidity up to a few too many drinks and an empowering feeling of being free and wild for the first time in her life. Since Chase had walked back into it, she'd acknowledged that maybe the strong sexual buzz he poured into her veins simply by occupying the same space might have been a contributing factor.

The alcohol she could handle—by eliminating it from her diet while Chase was around. The sexual attraction…that she couldn't seem to master. And the damn man knew it. She had no doubt that if he wanted to push her, she'd lose her mind and any hope of an annulment right along with it.

And she needed this annulment—for her career and her sanity. She wasn't the kind of woman who got married by accident by Elvis. That wasn't who she wanted to be.

Taking a cleansing breath, Rina closed her eyes and tried positive realization. She pictured in her mind how the next five minutes would go. And they did not include anything resembling kissing, groping, or wild, mindless sex.

She just hoped her body was paying attention to the command.

Walking to his front door, she squared her shoulders, straightened her spine and rang his bell.

"Sabrina."

"Rina."

He grinned at her, ignoring the correction. That superior turn of his lips was like nails along a blackboard. It bothered her more than his stubborn use of her full name.

"Can I come in?"

"Absolutely."

Stepping back, he motioned her inside. The door snicked shut behind her, nothing loud or unusual, but for the first time in her life she began to appreciate how convicts must feel the first time they entered that cell. She felt trapped, aroused and out of her element.

Clearing her throat, she pushed the feeling away. It was silly. She was a grown woman, a capable woman, with an excellent job she was good at and a life she was proud of. And once this was taken care of she could have it back.

"Nice place."

"Thanks. It doesn't quite feel like home yet."

"It will."

"Maybe." He shrugged. Something about his expression seemed…off. Or maybe it was the way he'd said the single word—like her father when he was just humoring one of her "girlie" tendencies.

"Can I offer you a beer?"

"Er, no thanks."

He stood there, staring at her, making her feel itchy and warm all at the same time. There was something about his intensity. She remembered having it entirely focused on her, on her pleasure. And she couldn't help but want that again.

Heat settled at the juncture of her thighs, smoldering and roiling.

He crossed the space between them. Rina took an instinctive step backward, her knees hitting squarely on the edge of his coffee table. If he hadn't reached out and grabbed her, she'd have sat right down on the glass-topped surface.

Real graceful.

"I, ah, wanted to apologize to you. I should have asked for your version of the events. I just didn't want to upset you."

"I know that."

Instead of letting her go like she expected, he brushed a single finger up and down the length of her arm. She shivered at the innocent caress. No. Spinning out of his grasp, she winced as her knees connected with the edge of the table again.

"Do I make you nervous?"

"Yes. No." Rina closed her eyes for a moment of strength, wishing she could erase the past few moments. Opening them, she looked into his dark blue eyes and answered truthfully. "A little."

"You've never been nervous around me before."

"Things were…different."

"How different could things be?"

Oh, if he only knew.

The twinkle of mischief and laughter that brightened his eyes made her smile automatically in return. She'd forgotten that. How he could make her smile with nothing more than one of his own. Seeing him enjoying himself had always made the world seem a little brighter, a little lighter.

"We're obviously still attracted to each other. Are you seeing anyone?"

"No." Rina shook her head slowly, realizing he'd given her the perfect barrier that her damn sense of honor wouldn't allow her to exploit.

She couldn't lie to him and say she was seeing some-one…not when she was going to tell him she was his wife. Their marriage might not be a real one, but she'd taken a vow—no matter that she hadn't realized she was doing it. He might not appreciate it or even expect it, but as far as she was concerned, until they had this little problem taken care of she'd made a promise to him that she would keep.

Which made the churning fire in her gut even harder to ignore. It had been a long time….

"Maybe we should sit down."

"Maybe you should tell me why you came over here, because something tells me it isn't the reason I was hoping for."

"No, it isn't to have sex."

"Are you sure?"

Chase moved a step closer into her personal space. The scent of musk and sandalwood came with him, along with the heat of his body. Her own body seemed to recognize him immediately, and the pulsing ache increased.

His hands burrowed into her hair, his fingers cupping the back of her head. His thumbs traced the line of her jaw before dipping down over the sensitive side of her neck to the curve of her collarbone. A shiver started from the touch of his thumbs to race down the length of her body.

Her lips parted. She felt their reluctant separation, as if some part of her was fighting against the unwanted reaction, even if most of her couldn't seem to resist.

Her breath sped up. She could feel it, somehow warmer than usual, flowing in and out of her lungs. Her body hummed, with anticipation, fear and the sense of a lost battle.

He hadn't even kissed her and she was a goner. Not that it mattered. Not at this moment. She wanted his kiss. Wanted it more strongly than anything else she could ever remember.

No sooner had the thought flitted through her mind than he obliged. His lips touched hers in a light caress that did little to assuage the need pounding through her. It only made her hungrier.

So she took, grabbing his retreating head and pulling him back to her mouth. She dived into him, fingers digging into his scalp, tongue sparring with his. Standing on tiptoe, she molded their bodies together simply for the pleasure of feeling his war-hardened muscles against her own.

A groan vibrated through his throat and his hands turned as demanding and expectant as hers, running up and down her spine, over her arms, latching on to her ass.

She arched her head back in surrender as his mouth traveled down her exposed throat. His hands flicked open the buttons on her lightweight top as his mouth sucked and licked a trail of fire down her neck, across her shoulders and toward her aching breasts.

She felt breathless, rushed and eager. She was mindless, the world hazy except for the clarity of sensation where he touched her. She throbbed. She wanted. She yearned for more.

Chase dropped to his knees at her feet, his fingers working the buttons of her jeans. His hands slipped inside, reaching around to cup her rear and pull her closer to him. Her fingers speared into his hair, twisting the military-short strands, needing something solid to hold her to reality.

He stared up at her from the V of her opened jeans; his eyes were dark and dilated with a passion that made her feel more powerful and alive than she had in months. Years. Ever.

She'd only ever come close to this feeling with him....

Reality slammed in like a ton of bricks hitting pavement.

Chase bowed his head to kiss the white lace triangle covering her sex. The warmth of his breath seeped through the fabric, fracturing her thoughts for a fragile second.

Then the jagged pieces came back together, poking into her conscience and spurring her to action.

"No, Chase. Stop. We can't have sex." Her hands pushed against his shoulders, slipping off before finally finding purchase.

"Why not?"

"Because we're married."

6

"WHAT DID YOU SAY?"

The floor rocked beneath Chase's knees, the sensation eerily similar to the moment of takeoff, that split second right as aerodynamics take over. He stared up at her, those lush green eyes and kiss-swollen lips, and wanted nothing more than to ignore her words. To pretend he hadn't heard them. To surrender them both to the unbelievable storm of desire he'd been fighting since the moment he'd seen her again.

"We're married."

But he couldn't do that. "How is that possible?"

His voice echoed against the naked white walls as he climbed to his feet and moved away, away from temptation and her words.

Straightening her clothes, she reached for her purse—he hadn't even noticed she'd carried one when she'd landed on his doorstep—and pulled out a sheaf of papers.

"That was exactly what I thought when this arrived in the mail." She separated a sheet from the stack and thrust it at him.

He stared down at a marriage certificate, complete with his name, her name and a bunch of scrolling curlicues around the edges that he supposed were meant to be romantic. They weren't.

"Is this real?"

"Unfortunately."

The room rocked again, almost as if his apartment had started pulling Gs.

"How did this happen?"

"We were both a little drunk and didn't pay attention to the fact that they also did real weddings. Apparently, when we asked for the Elvis wedding neither one of us made it clear we wanted the fake one so they assumed we were there for the real thing instead of the punk-your-friends version."

"Don't you need a marriage license…" His voice trailed off as he remembered the sheets of paper they'd filled out. Without the fog of alcohol, he realized how weird it was to have to give all that information for fake photos.

"Yep. We signed in front of a notary who took care of all the details for us. Part of the complete package, apparently."

He stared at her, uncertain what to say. There was no protocol for this kind of situation. Rolling around inside his head was a jumble of emotions—shock, anger, confusion. At the center of them, though, was desire. No matter what, he wanted this woman. And probably always would.

"It could have been worse. I could have gotten pregnant."

Chase frowned at her. "That isn't even funny."

"I'm sorry. I know it isn't. I just meant that this is something that can be fixed."

"Fixed? You mean a divorce?" His lips pulled into an unintended sneer on the word. It was the last thing he'd ever wanted. Not after the disaster his parents had turned into.

"Annulment. It's the legal equivalent of turning back time."

"Great. Fantastic." Chase heard the sarcasm in his own words. Raking a hand across his scalp, he stared down at the piece of paper in his hand, reading each and every syllable several times just to let them all sink in.

His mind raced…remembered. And he groaned. "We were married by Elvis."

Sabrina laughed. She honest to God laughed. Not just laughed but collapsed onto his couch in a fit of laughter that had tears streaming across her cheeks.

Chase stared down at her, not entirely sure what to do with her. "I'm glad you think this is so funny."

Swiping at tears, she looked up at him from her prone position on his sofa. Despite everything, he couldn't prevent the flitting image of her there, naked, beneath him.

"Not funny. Trust me. I've just spent the past eleven months worrying about how you were going to take this and all you can think about is that *Elvis* married us."

Chase straightened to his full height. "Well, it isn't exactly how I pictured getting married."

"I shudder at the thought of you picturing it at all."

Something she'd said finally registered in his mind. "Eleven months. You've known about this for eleven months?"

"Yes, that—" she pointed at the piece of paper still wobbling in his hand "—arrived in my mailbox about a week later."

"A week? You've known about this for that long and didn't think you should tell me? Call me? Write me a goddamn letter?"

Blood began to fill his head; he could feel it pounding behind his ears. His chest tightened. How could she have kept something this important from him?

"How? I couldn't very well send you a letter about something like this. *Dear Chase, by the way, we're married.* Calling was out of the question. Something like this deserved face-to-face time. Besides, it wasn't worth the risk of someone else finding out. That's the last thing we need."

"What do you mean?"

"I mean it could end both our careers if anyone in the air force finds out that we're married. We're both guilty of fraud."

He wasn't certain how to feel. How to react. What to say or think. Part of him wanted to grab Sabrina and shake her. Another part wanted to pull her into his arms and claim her as his so that no one—not the air force, not the General, not even Sabrina—could take her away from him again. That, more than anything, was what scared the hell out of him.

"Well, excuse me for not reasoning this whole thing through quickly enough for you, Sabrina. But apparently *you've* had eleven months to figure out the repercussions while *I've* only had about five minutes."

Her response was a thinning of her lips and a narrowing of her eyes. He didn't appreciate the implication that some-how he was at fault in this situation.

"I deserved to know, Sabrina." His words were low and dangerous. She'd been the one making decisions about his life without even informing him that they needed to be made.

She stood up from the couch, unafraid to ignore his warn-ing, uncompromising as she stood toe-to-toe with him, de-fending her choice. "Yes. But not like that."

There was fire in her eyes, anger mixed with something that sparked a primitive response in his already racing blood.

He moved closer, nothing more than the subtle leaning of his body to hers. But her immediate response was to take a step back. Her eyes, hard emerald-green, tore straight through him, and left him feeling off balance and…wrong.

Chase followed as she retreated. He wasn't entirely sure why. Perhaps it was the need to regain some semblance of control over the situation.

She stopped only when her back hit the wall with a quiet thud. His body was flush with hers. Her scent surrounded him, a mixture of strawberries and sex, innocence and sinful sur-render.

He stared into her, the urge to take everything she could

give strong and powerful. His eyes latched onto her lips, pink, plump from their earlier kisses, and inviting—even if she hadn't meant them to be.

Her tongue licked across them. Need knifed through him.

But instead of voicing an invitation, "Stop" fell from her parted lips. The single whispered word held none of the conviction it had minutes before when she'd demanded the same thing. And yet it doused him just as surely as if she'd screamed it.

Moving away, Chase pulled in lungfuls of air and sanity. "Why did you wait?"

Her chest rose and fell in a hurried rhythm that matched his own. "I told you."

Somehow the fact that she was as affected as he helped him find his control.

"No. Why didn't you tell me that first day? That first night?"

"Oh sure. It's great to have you back from the war. Glad you survived since it would have been a pain in my ass to have to explain about the wife you didn't even know about."

"Sarcasm doesn't—" Chase stopped mid-sentence, interrupted by a knock on his front door. "What the hell…"

"Ignore it. This is more important." The irritation in Sabrina's voice matched his own, part arousal, part exasperation. It set his teeth—and his nerves—on edge.

"No." He couldn't. Only a handful of people knew where he lived. Not that he appreciated the ill-timed interruption. Whoever it was would be leaving immediately.

Yanking the door open, Chase looked around on his front stoop. No one was there. This was a bad time for the teenagers in the neighborhood to start playing pranks.

He was about to turn back into the room when a flutter of something white at his feet caught his eyes. Bending down, he slowly picked it up.

He knew exactly what it was, the twin to the note that currently lay on the desk in his office. Only this one carried no stamp, no postmark. This one had been hand delivered.

Ripping it open, he stared down at the black letters.

Cancel the ceremony or you'll regret the consequences.

No joke. He already regretted them.

"What is that?"

Stuffing the note and envelope into his pocket, Chase turned back to Sabrina. "Nothing." He wouldn't, couldn't, deal with this now.

She stared at him for a moment before turning her eyes to study his empty white walls.

Without looking at him she said quietly, "I wanted to have the annulment paperwork ready before I said anything. I figured it would be easier that way."

"Easier on whom? Certainly not me."

"Don't be stupid. That's your male pride talking. You're just angry that I kept this from you."

"Hell, yes. I'm angry."

How had this turned to shit so quickly? He'd been married for all of five minutes and they were already bickering like his parents had before their divorce.

He supposed it was fitting.

"Look, I'm simply saying I don't like being kept in the dark about events that concern my life."

"Yeah, well neither do I. I didn't even know where you were for eleven months. I had to find out about the fact that you'd almost died on the news like everyone else."

The accusation in her words stunned him. What the hell? "I had no idea you were my wife, Sabrina." He ground out the words through clenched teeth. "Or that you cared. You were the one who left in the middle of the night, remember?"

She stared at him for several moments. Chase watched the cool and perfect veneer slip over her from head to toe; it fell like a film of silk, hiding the emotions and woman beneath. Her spine pulled straight, adding an inch to her slight frame, and her green eyes blanked of everything.

"I don't. Care. I'll leave what I have. Take a look. My phone number's on the first page."

Chase watched her walk away, standing at his window as she sank stiffly into her compact car and left.

THAT HADN'T GONE the way she'd hoped. Rina sat in the parking space outside her apartment, staring through the windshield. She hadn't moved from the spot since she'd pulled into it five minutes before.

On a scale of one to ten, it had been about negative two. Yes, she could have handled things a little better. She'd picked the worst possible moment to tell him, that was for sure. But Chase could have handled things better as well.

She hated fighting with him.

But she hated the edge of needy weakness she'd let slip through at the end more. She didn't care about him. Not really. Not more than any normal, sane person would have cared about someone they knew who was now living, working, eating every day in a war zone.

How many nights had she spent lying awake, unable to sleep, picturing the danger he was in, the moment he might die?

And she'd been angry with him for putting her in that position. She hadn't asked for it. She'd never wanted to date a pilot, let alone marry one. She'd had plenty of experience wondering if or when her father would come home. That fear, the fear of being left alone, of losing the one and only person she depended on, had finally gone away when her father had taken a desk job and given up flying. She never wanted to be that vulnerable again.

It had been bad enough when she'd found out the danger Chase had been in *after* the fact.

Of course, she was partly to blame. It was her own fault, her own mistake. But knowing that hadn't taken away the fear. It had only added guilt to the pile.

Pushing the heels of her hands into her stinging eyes, Rina rubbed the sensation away. She had no right to cry over Chase. Certainly not now that he was safe. And home.

She wondered briefly what that white card he'd stuffed into his pocket had been about. Probably a note from some woman for the Babe Magnet.

Ha. Could her life get any more screwed up?

At least the worst part was over. She'd told him. Chase had the paperwork. So why didn't she feel better about the whole thing?

CHASE LOOKED down at the papers in his hands again. The annulment documents were in his right and the note card in his left.

He couldn't see the words. All he could see were pictures of Sabrina flashing across his mind. Blazing clear images of the night they'd…married. The way she'd tugged the edge of her uniform his first day with the squadron. The feel of her up against the wall of his bare apartment.

Fate. He'd never been a huge believer. Good fortune was what happened when you worked hard, not what simply landed in your lap. Of course, being in a war zone had a way of changing your views on fate and faith.

Watching men die had a way of changing your outlook on life.

He might not have meant to marry Sabrina, but he couldn't shake the feeling that it had happened for a reason. Had he really not known what was going on? Or had he not wanted to stop it? Had he wanted to leave knowing she'd be home, waiting for him?

Was he ready to let that go? To let her go without taking some time to think about things? Evaluate what they'd done? What they had?

Growing up, he'd sworn he'd never get married unless he knew it was forever. He'd never put his children through the hell of divorce the way his parents had. They'd given up on each other, but he'd been the one to pay the price.

Being a pilot took him away for days, weeks, sometimes months at a time, hard enough on a family with strong ties. He'd be damned if he'd let his children end up halfway across the country, hours away, with no time to see them and no way to be a part of their lives.

He'd gone years between strained visits with his father. The last time he'd seen the man he'd been fourteen. When he'd needed him most, his father hadn't been there. And then he'd been gone, dead of a heart attack. For years he'd blamed his mother. But that wasn't entirely fair.

She hadn't been happy with his father. He'd known that. But Chase hadn't been happy without him. While his mother and sister had grown closer, Chase had floundered. They had each other, he had no one. What he remembered most about his teenage years was the unbelievable feeling of loneliness and loss. He never wanted to experience that again.

He'd joined the air force, surrounded himself with a brotherhood of men who'd bonded over shared experiences and a sense of honor and duty. He'd made lifelong friendships that only death could take away.

He'd never felt that same sense of...of connection with

any woman. Until Sabrina. He'd glimpsed an inkling of it when they'd been together those brief few weeks seven years before. He'd experienced it full force eleven months ago when they'd connected on much more than a physical level— at least he had.

A sense of connection that for him had only intensified during his months away.

He'd married Sabrina. He'd made a vow—a vow he didn't realize he was making but a vow just the same. Surely that meant something. They certainly had plenty of sexual chemistry in their favor.

He wasn't ready to simply throw it all away.

Yes, she was right that it had the potential to screw up both of their careers. But he thought that she was overreacting. He seriously doubted the air force would prosecute them. It was more a mistake, an accident, than intentional fraud. He was a war hero about to be awarded the Distinguished Flying Cross in front of the President. The air force didn't need the kind of scandal that prosecuting him would create.

Besides, Sabrina was worth the risk. He'd give up a hell of a lot to have her in his life. So they'd skipped a few steps and jumped straight to an unintentional marriage.

Making a decision, Chase tapped the pages neatly together and placed them in the bottom drawer of his desk. He wasn't going to give up on his relationship with Sabrina without at least trying to make it work. A few weeks. A month maybe. If, after that, things weren't working out, then at least their divorce wouldn't affect anyone besides him and Sabrina. And he'd know. He wouldn't ask himself twenty years from now, *what if?*

His gaze switched to the note card in his other hand. The paper was crumpled now, not as crisp and perfect as it had been lying on his concrete porch.

The fact that it had been there at all unnerved him a little. Whoever was sending these notes was close. Knew where he lived, not just the abstract address on an envelope, but had stood on his front porch, possibly looked through his front window and watched as he and Sabrina had argued.

He didn't like that at all.

And he didn't like being given an ultimatum, especially by a coward unwilling to confront him in person. As much as he'd like to cancel the medal ceremony, that simply wasn't going to happen.

But he also couldn't ignore the note this time. This was a concrete threat to himself and the air force. He had a few ideas as to who might be unhappy with him receiving a medal. There'd been a few army guys not happy with the attention he'd received, and a couple of outspoken family members who'd been consumed with grief. He'd start digging there and see what shook out.

In the meantime he'd concentrate on Sabrina. That was infinitely more pleasant. The question was how to convince her to give them a chance. She was a thoroughly stubborn woman. Once she made up her mind…it was difficult to change it. Not that he wasn't up to the challenge. Their marriage had taken less than ten minutes. The decision to end it should take much longer.

"WHY CAN'T WE have sex?"

Sabrina nearly had a heart attack at the sound of Chase's voice at her office door. She did actually jump in her chair. And then hated herself for the startled reaction.

The heat spilling through her body was adrenaline. It had absolutely nothing to do with the fact that he had shut the door behind him, blocking out the rest of the world from her tiny space. Chase leaned his back against the wood, one hand still holding the knob as if to lock her there, with him.

"What?" The word croaked through her suddenly dry throat, completely and totally someone else's voice.

What the hell was wrong with her? All the man had to do was say the word *sex* and her mind turned to mush.

"No." She shook her head, hoping that at least one of them would heed her words, but she wasn't entirely certain she had the strength for it to be her. "No, no, no, no, no."

He smiled, that charm-filled, amped-up, wicked smile that had her resolve melting and her intelligence dripping to her toes.

She hadn't heard from him in two days. Not one single word since she'd left the papers with him on Friday. And now, the first thing he had to say to her was "Why can't we have sex?"

"No." The word came out much stronger this time. Thank heaven for small miracles. "Sex would ruin the annulment. If we have sex, then we can't claim that we haven't been living as husband and wife."

"No one has to know."

"I'll know."

Rina watched his smile fade. She didn't understand the momentary look of regret that flashed across his winter-blue eyes.

"Look, Sabrina—"

"Rina."

Chase lifted an eyebrow at her. "Sabrina. From what I've read, the eleven months we've waited might be enough of a problem to prevent the annulment anyway."

"Yes, but according to my lawyer the extenuating circumstances are probably sufficient to jump that hurdle."

"And if they aren't?"

Rina's stomach took a nosedive at the mere thought. "Then we get a divorce. It'll be more difficult but…"

"But that would take longer and the chances of someone finding out get better."

"Exactly."

"Remind me again what happens if someone finds out? I mean, there's no requirement that says we can't have a relationship or get married."

"Are you willing to risk a letter of reprimand? Are you willing to risk the possibility that we'll be booted from the program, ruin any forward momentum our careers have and never get another promotion again? I'm not. I have plans and ambitions, goals. I do not intend to reach the peak of my air force career at twenty-nine!"

Chase stared down at her, watching the way her breasts moved up and down with each of her labored breaths. Awareness rolled through her, along with the desire to cross her arms over her chest and block his view for both of their sakes.

"You know, I'm not so sure your reluctance to let anyone know about our marriage has anything to do with the repercussions to your job."

"What are you talking about?"

"I think maybe you're more afraid that the General might find out."

Rina's eyes narrowed. She did not like his tone of voice. "Excuse me for not wanting anyone, including my father, to find out that I accidentally married an idiot."

"What does that make you?"

"Excuse me?"

He sauntered across her suddenly claustrophobic office, stopping at the corner of her desk. "If I'm an idiot, what does that make you, the woman who accidentally married me?"

She looked up into his face, into his deep blue eyes full of self-deprecating humor. Part of her wanted to be mad at him for not taking their predicament seriously. But part of her was relieved that he was apparently no longer angry at her for not telling him right away.

"A moron?"

"Hmm. You'd think we'd be perfect for each other. It's enlightening to know your opinion of me as a husband."

His knowing smile was back, and so was the pit in the bottom of her stomach. She seriously hoped he couldn't see the pulse beating double time in her throat. "I don't really have a husband, do I?"

"That's not what the pretty piece of paper I have says."

Rina moved her head sideways and smiled. In the face of his teasing, she couldn't help it. Smiling about this situation was the last thing she'd expected to be able to do. But it felt good. Certainly better than worrying alone.

Dropping his hand, Chase took a step away and said, "Look. If we can't be lovers, we might as well be friends. We're stuck with each other at least for a few more weeks."

Something the General had told her as a teenager surfaced in her mind. *Boys only want one thing from a girl and it sure as hell isn't friendship.*

Although, Chase was right. They were stuck with each other. As long as he understood the no-sex rule and seemed to want the annulment…and why wouldn't he?

She always felt, acted, *was* different around him. And she liked it. She had no idea why, but he made her feel…wild. Free. For the first time in a very long time. He made her question the decisions she'd made for herself.

It wasn't that she'd been *unhappy* before. She just hadn't realized there could be more. The sad part was it couldn't last.

But what was the harm in enjoying it until the annulment came through? As long as she could keep her libido under control. "No sex?"

"Not unless you offer."

7

CHASE SLIPPED inside Sabrina's office, closing the door quietly behind him. He knew from talking to one of her staff that she'd had a meeting with the local news station about promoting his ceremony this morning. He had no idea how long she'd be gone, but he'd wanted to get into her office for the past several days and hadn't had the chance before now. She had a lot going on with coordinating all the elements of his ceremony—catering, Secret Service, security for everyone else. She'd barely left her office, either staring at her computer or talking on the telephone.

What he wanted should be easy to find. Sabrina was picky and efficient if nothing else. He'd guarantee she had file folders labeled and cross-referenced neatly in her desk for every task she could possibly be expected to tackle. He just hoped she hadn't taken the information he wanted with her.

Sitting down at her desk, the scent of her wafted up from the worn leather to surround him. Strawberries and sin. He couldn't stop the automatic smile that thought brought.

Shaking his head, he reached for her desk drawer and pulled it open. Right up front, right on top, nondescript manila with a perfect white label, Chase Carden Medal Ceremony.

Pulling it out, he laid it across her desk and opened the cover. It was a big file, with several sections. He flipped to one that was labeled Invitations, and held his breath.

Just as he'd hoped, the info he'd wanted was there. The list of all the families he'd asked her to invite, the ones who'd lost loved ones that night. The mere thought had a hard knot forming in his stomach. Clenching his teeth, he forced it away.

He quickly pulled the pages out, used her desktop all-in-one to make a copy and placed everything back where it had been.

At least he now had a starting point. Jackhammer was looking discreetly into the active-duty army personnel who'd been outspoken about their anger at not having received the same level of recognition as he had. And he was going to look into these families.

Who knew what he'd find, but at least it was a starting point.

He stood up, folded the papers, placed them in his pocket and headed for the door. Before he could reach for it, it opened.

"What are you doing here?"

He stared at Sabrina as she entered her office, frowning at him.

"Waiting for you. What are you doing this weekend?"

Her frown deepened, but he continued to ignore her obvious puzzlement at his presence.

She answered slowly, "Nothing," as if trying to figure out where the land mine lay and how to avoid it.

"I wanted to ask a favor. I need a female opinion on something for my apartment."

"And I was the best choice?"

"More like the only choice."

She snorted, an unladylike sound that clashed wonderfully with her perfectly polished exterior.

"I believe that, Babe Magnet."

"Believe whatever you want. I'm tired of looking at four milk-white walls, but I suck at picking out colors and crap. I need someone with a sense of visual awareness."

"And you think I can help? You've never seen my place. Maybe the walls are painted lime-green."

"First of all, I've seen the graphic layouts you do for the squadron—you have a very artistic eye. And I happen to like green, any shade, although the color your eyes turn when you climax would be my favorite." He smiled. He simply couldn't help himself. "Besides, I suspect red, white and blue covers every surface of your apartment."

She ignored his provoking statements, and asked, "Why me?"

"Because despite what you seem to think, there aren't a lot of women in my life and the men I know would skin me alive if I even asked…friend."

Chase watched the war within patiently, she fought a battle he knew he'd win. She was attracted to him, whether she wanted to admit it or not. She liked spending time with him, a fact he couldn't find fault with. He *was* rather charming.

And she had a whimsical, creative streak she tried hard to hide, a streak she rarely let run free…just like the passionate side of her personality he seemed to be the only person aware of. She put up such a front with everyone around her, all the while concealing the most exciting and intriguing elements of her personality.

Her eyes narrowed to slits of glimmering green but in the end she agreed, as he knew she would.

"Fine. I'll help, but only for a few hours."

"Fantastic. I'll pick you up at eight tomorrow morning and we can hit Lowe's."

"Eight?"

"Don't even try to pretend. You're a creature of habit, Sabrina." He ignored her sigh of annoyance. "You get up at the butt crack of dawn every day. I'm giving you an extra hour to sleep in." Chase took a quick scan around, checking to make sure they were alone before invading her personal space just enough to make her squirm. "And this time don't use it to sneak away."

RINA STOOD at the front window to her apartment, well behind the drapes so Chase couldn't see her, and waited for him to show. She honestly had no idea what she was doing. Making a colossal mistake obviously, but aside from that…

He pulled into a spot in front of her place. Before he could even get completely out of the car she'd grabbed her purse, locked her door and was standing on the sidewalk waiting for him.

She didn't want to let him inside her space. Somehow that felt too intimate for her peace of mind, like a line that, once crossed, she wouldn't be able to push them back over.

"Ready?"

Without waiting for his answer, Rina opened the passenger door to his sleek black Mustang and slid inside. She was immediately enveloped by Chase, his scent, his presence, his heat.

Her own internal temperature rose in response and she squirmed on the leather seat, trying to find some relief from the pressure spiking inside.

"Lowe's, Home Depot, the furniture store. Any secret female destinations for making a house a home?"

"Michaels. The craft store."

She'd said it more to torture him than anything. She'd honestly thought he'd balk at the suggestion. The image of him towering over displays of silk flowers, picture frames and glass beads made her smile and put her back on an even keel.

Until he said, "Okay, and Michaels."

"No, I—"

He cranked the car and music blared from the speakers, drowning out her protest. Shrugging, Rina figured getting the visual in living color would be her payment for the hours of self-torture she'd agreed to.

But what she'd thought would be the longest morning of her life turned out to be almost fun.

Whenever she and the General had moved to a new place, Rina had always tried to make it feel like home. She'd never quite succeeded, partly because no place had ever really been *home* but mostly because the General hadn't cared what color the walls were painted as long as the house was spotless. He ordered her not to clutter up the place with frills like picture frames or throw pillows. The only spot that she'd ever been able to truly make her own had been her bedroom. As long as she kept everything in its place he'd let her "girlie" it up.

But Chase wasn't anything like the General. Either he was blowing a butt load of smoke up her ass or he was genuinely interested in paint chips, wallpaper borders and sconces. However, she did completely bypass the silk flower section... Even she wasn't that cruel.

They ended up at the furniture store since the other stores were located closer together. Walking in the door, she still wasn't quite certain what their agenda was.

"What are we looking for?"

"Whatever I like."

"You already have an apartment full of furniture."

"How do you know that? You only saw one room."

True, but she couldn't imagine that he only had one room furnished. Besides... "I thought you said all the stuff had come from storage."

"It did. But I sold several things before I left. I figured after being locked up in a musty room for months there were certain things I'd want to replace."

"Like what?"

Standing on tiptoe, Rina looked over the vast sea of furniture laid out in the humongous warehouse before them. The place was huge. How would they ever find anything if he wouldn't tell her what he was looking for?

She was so engrossed in surveying the place that she didn't even notice he'd moved closer until his words brushed against the skin at the nape of her neck.

"Like a bed."

A shiver of unwanted anticipation rushed down her spine. Her body shuddered. She couldn't help it.

"Goose walk across your grave?" Chase ran his hand down her arm.

Jerking away, she threw him a look that should have had him taking ten paces back. He simply smiled down at her knowingly.

"May I help you?"

Sure, now a salesman showed up. Where had he been three minutes ago?

"We're looking for a new bed."

"He. He's looking for a new bed. I'm just along for the ride."

Both men turned to stare, Chase calling her on her words with nothing more than a look and the salesman turning rather red-faced.

Clearing his throat, the other man asked, "Are you looking for something in particular? Four-poster? Sleigh? Dark or light wood?"

"Big's my only requirement."

Rina trailed behind the men as they set off through the store.

"We can order any of the designs in a king so size isn't an issue."

Rina muffled her snort with a cough, but when Chase

turned back to look at her she had a feeling he knew exactly what had crossed her mind. Size was always an issue when men were involved, not that Chase was anything to snort at. The man embodied *king-size* in every possible way.

She simply smiled angelically. And tried to get her mind out of the gutter. A difficult endeavor staring at his tight ass, remembering it filling the palms of her hands as he thrust deep inside her. What was wrong with her? If she couldn't control her thoughts she had next to no hope of controlling her impulses. Considering that every minute she and Chase spent together those impulses seemed to get bigger, stronger, more difficult to deny...

"What do you like?"

Pulling herself back to reality, she said, "It doesn't matter what I like. It's your bed."

"But I want to know what you think."

"I think you're wasting good money. I find it hard to believe that your bedroom doesn't already have a bed."

"I've decided I need something brand-new, something no one has shared with me."

He slipped a finger into a curl that had fallen from the clip she'd scraped her hair back with. She knew she should have pulled the mess up like usual.

"Yet."

The word was for her alone and had her heart beating loudly in her chest. Suddenly, the room felt warm, her clothes tight and constricting to her skin.

Clearing her throat—and the sensation—away, she said, "I like that one," and pointed to the first bedroom display she saw.

It was a modified sleigh bed, dark cherry wood with a vine pattern carved around the edge. It felt intimate and...sexy somehow. Or maybe that was just the leftover hormones pumping through her blood.

Chase moved to the center of the decorated display. He stood, studying the space for a good five minutes without saying anything, turning every few moments to view another piece of the bedroom suite.

"I'll take it."

"Which pieces, sir?"

"All of it. I want every accent piece, lamp, bookend, and I want the bed as big as you can get it."

Rina watched the salesman's eyes widen before filling with dollar signs.

Walking up beside Chase, she nudged him and grumbled out the side of her mouth, "I think he works on commission."

He smiled down at her, not his usual smile but something softer, more real. She jerked her hand away from his arm and stepped backward into the dresser. The mirror rocked with a loud squeak and heat flooded her face.

"I'm such a klutz."

"No you're not. But it's nice to know I can fluster you."

"Of course you don't."

"Why don't the two of you go over to our mattress gallery while I write up the rest of the order?"

Without hesitation, Chase grabbed her hand and headed in that direction, pulling her reluctantly along behind him.

"You didn't even look at a single price tag. Aren't you worried about how much this is all going to cost?"

"No. I inherited some insurance money when my father died eight years ago. I've had no reason to spend any of it until now."

Rina stopped dead in her tracks, yanking back on their joined hands. Someone had to talk some sense into the man. Just because he had money to throw around didn't mean he had to throw it away. Besides, she didn't like the way he'd said *father,* tight and controlled. In fact, it was the first time Chase had ever mentioned the man to her.

"Seriously, Chase. Are you sure you need everything over there? I mean if you really want some bookends then we can head to Target after this. It'll cost a hell of a lot less."

"But it will require more time than I'm willing to give. I have a better idea on how we can spend the rest of the day."

"Oh yeah. Like what?"

Using their linked hands against her, he pulled her across the space separating them until she was less than an inch from his chest. His eyes glowed down at her, full of a desire her flesh distinctly remembered, even if her mind had tried very hard to forget.

Her lips parted. It wasn't an invitation. Really it wasn't. She just couldn't get enough oxygen into her lungs. Into her brain. Everything seemed to turn a little fuzzy at the edges. It all blurred away, everything but the glow of Chase's eyes staring into her own as he said in a low, rumbling voice, "Painting."

CHASE RELISHED the way her pupils dilated, the way her pink lips parted, the way her body leaned into his, closing the gap between them even as he knew she really didn't want to.

God, she was fighting hard. However, she was going to lose. Today. Tomorrow. Next week. It didn't matter. Sabrina McAllister, no, Sabrina Carden, wanted him. Almost as much as he wanted her.

Now it was simply a matter of convincing her to listen to her body and let go. Somehow, he didn't think letting go was very easy for her.

Of course, that just meant that when she finally did, the moment would be unbelievable. He'd had a taste of that experience on their wedding night. Only it wasn't enough. He wanted that again. He wanted more.

Chase unconsciously tightened his grip on her hand as his already snug jeans strangled his erection.

"Ouch," she protested, tugging away from his hold.

Just as well. Throwing her down on one of the display mattresses probably wouldn't have won him any brownie points.

"Mattress first, though." His voice started out as gravel before he cleared it away.

They entered the small section, a sea of snow-white mattresses just waiting for someone to jump in. He was a firm believer in comfort and had no problem paying to ensure he slept well. As a pilot, he couldn't afford to spend the entire night tossing and turning because his mattress was too soft or too stiff. He needed to be alert and focused. He'd learned firsthand the price that could be paid if he wasn't.

Flopping onto the first one, he tested it out.

"Too hard."

He watched Sabrina as he moved from one display to the next, her cheeks flaming an adorable, rosy pink that matched his memory of her aroused nipples. Her muscles were strung so taut he thought she might snap.

"Why don't you lie down? Try this one." Relax.

"No, I'm good here." Her voice ground out the protest.

Finally, she did walk to the other end of the room, as far from him as possible, and lay down on a mattress. Apparently, she was more comfortable away from him. No, *comfortable* wasn't the right word, because he could still see the tension tightening her body from here. The sexual awareness snapped between them.

He watched her as he moved methodically from one mattress to the other, keeping her always in his sights. It was just as well that she'd put space between them—even if it wouldn't change the eventual outcome. His body still hadn't cooled down and wasn't likely to with her standing between him and a bed.

After about five minutes he narrowed down his choices, calling her over.

"Sabrina. What do you think about this one?"

She wove through the displays to his side, standing just far enough away that he couldn't reach out and grab her.

Chase looked up at her from his prone position; her body was as stiff as the forest of shellacked and painted wood inside the place.

Rolling his eyes, he reared up and grabbed her hand, pulling her down onto the soft pillow top beside him. He honestly wanted her opinion since he seriously hoped she'd be sharing the mattress with him at some point.

She landed with a decidedly unfeminine grunt, sprawling across his body in a way that sorely tempted his control and restraint. But she didn't give him a chance to act on the impulses firing through his brain. Take. Plunder. Own.

She squirmed away from him as if he were the newest case of bird flu, kneeing him painfully in the upper thigh in the process. A small price to pay, he supposed. It sure as hell could have been worse. He narrowed his eyes, considering whether or not it had been an accident.

Letting his hands drop to his sides, empty unfortunately, he said, "Lay down for heaven's sake. I'm not going to jump you in the middle of the showroom floor."

"You're not going to jump me at all."

The force behind her words had a smile playing at his lips. He heard the uncertainty behind her statement, even if she hadn't wanted him to.

There was a distinct possibility that he might jump her this damn second if he couldn't get control. His erection pulsed painfully against the hard line of his fly, obvious for anyone who wanted to look—including Sabrina.

She wasn't helping him much, either. He could practically feel the hum in her blood from here.

She tried to vault back up but he reached for her hand,

holding her in place. After struggling in vain against him for a minute she finally gave up and with a flounce dropped flat to the mattress beside him.

"What do you think?"

"I think you promised we would be friends."

"Aren't we?"

She rolled her head sideways. The glare lost all of its power from that angle, but it sure as hell was cute to watch her try to be fierce.

"Look, I'm trying here. I can't deny that I'm attracted to you."

"Try a little harder."

Rolling his head away from her, he asked, "Can you see yourself sleeping on this?"

"Chase."

The one word was a warning, a warning he was probably going to ignore…even if he was lying on a mattress, the most vulnerable parts of his anatomy within easy striking distance.

"I just mean is it comfortable?"

"It doesn't matter. I'm not going to be sleeping on it."

"Rina, answer the damn question."

CHASE HAD seriously rattled her in that mattress room. He'd never called her Rina.

And for some reason she didn't like it.

Everyone in her life called her Rina. He was the only person who'd insisted on calling her Sabrina. Well, the only person since her mother. It had bothered her.

But hearing her nickname in his smooth, commanding voice had bothered her more. She'd needed to get out of there; away from him and the jumble of mixed-up emotions he made her feel.

One minute Rina had been adamant about going home.

She had things of her own to do…laundry, dusting, scrub-bing the toilet. Anything that would get her away from the temptation of her husband.

The next she'd found herself not only in Chase's living room arranging drop cloths on the hardwood floor, but also agreeing to come back and finish up the project tomorrow.

What the bloody hell was wrong with her?

No. She knew what was wrong with her. Hormones—and possibly his pheromones since she wasn't ready to take all the blame—were controlling her brain.

She knew what her problem was. What she couldn't figure out was what Chase's was. He was clearly torturing them both. But why? If he thought tumbling her onto the mattress beside him in the furniture store was enough to make her forget about the annulment and have sex with him, he was dead wrong. Hopefully.

"There. Everything's taped."

They'd first stopped by her apartment to pick up some old paint clothes. Running inside while she'd made him wait in the car, she'd pulled out the ugliest, rattiest, most holey long-sleeved T-shirt and cutoff jean shorts she could find. They were probably at least ten years old.

But the look of complete and utter devastation on Chase's face when she'd come out of her place was not what she'd hoped for. She'd wanted him to think twice about touching her…not be scared to death of her.

She would have turned on her heel to go back inside, if he hadn't stopped her. "Please promise me you'll never wear those clothes ever again."

"Why not? There's absolutely nothing wrong with these." She looked down. They covered everything, damn it. She knew how to dress herself. She'd been doing it for almost twenty-five years.

"Sure, if you're a man without a pulse. God, you have the most amazing legs. How am I supposed to concentrate on painting? Especially when I've had them wrapped around my waist, your heels dug into my thighs, urging me on."

She should have been incensed at his tone of voice and blatant words. Instead she'd felt powerful and…sexy. It was a feeling she relished for about three minutes, until she realized it only increased the ever-present pressure between her thighs.

Damn it! He hadn't even touched her.

But somehow she'd ignored both it and Chase, reclaiming her equilibrium and resolve somewhere in the monotony of spreading plastic and taping walls. Now the afternoon sun was setting outside the newly prepared windows, and she wasn't feeling so steady or certain…about anything.

"How about we start on that wall, get as much done right now, and then break for pizza in a couple hours."

"Oh, no. I'll just head home when we're done."

"No. You've sacrificed your entire Saturday and promised me Sunday. The least I can do is feed you."

His commanding tone of voice put her back up but she didn't argue. Somehow she thought maybe that was exactly what he wanted her to do. It had taken her a while to realize it, but her mind had needed to concentrate on something else as they'd worked silently together. Chase had been purposely baiting her all day. She had no idea why, but she also had no intention of falling in line with whatever he wanted… anymore.

For the next two hours she painted. Furiously. The skin across her shoulder blades felt tight enough to split down the center, spilling everything she was onto the floor at his feet. She was nervous and jacked up on adrenaline. She hated feeling this way, so out of control—of herself and the entire situation.

At the end of it all, her arms ached, her back ached and she groaned with relief that the torture of being in the same room with him was almost over. She wanted to go home, curl under the covers and just be. She'd make up some excuse for tomorrow, maybe come down with a sudden case of the flu. Or—or chicken pox.

"Pizza. What do you want on yours?"

"Just cheese."

Raising an eyebrow he said, "Pizza purist?"

"More like my pizza taste buds never grew up. There's something comforting and familiar about just plain cheese."

"Cheese it is."

He stepped into the kitchen. Rina stopped in the center of the room and waited for him to come back with a phone or coupons in his hand. When after a few minutes he hadn't, she started to get antsy. Her gaze darted from sheet-draped surfaces to fresh rolled paint. Her legs trembled with the urge to shift nervously back and forth. She fought it down.

"You want a beer? Glass of wine?"

"No thanks." Although the tightening in her stomach that seemed to appear at the mention of alcohol mixed with Chase didn't materialize, she still didn't think it would be the best choice. Especially considering how close to the edge of stupidity her hormones had her tilting. "Water would be great, though."

"Why don't you come in here? It'll be easier than yelling."

With one last, longing look toward the front door, Rina headed to the doorway off the far side of the room.

Instead of sitting at the table, looking through a phone book for the number like she'd expected, Chase stood at the counter, a ball of dough, a canning jar of red sauce and a pile of freshly grated cheeses in front of him.

"You're not ordering it from Pizza Hut?" Obviously.

"Sacrilege. No one makes better pizza than my mother, especially not that place. She'd die before she'd send her son into a cruel world without teaching him the art of a homemade pie."

"Are you guys Italian?"

"No. She just knew how to make a killer pizza."

Sitting down on one of the stools at the island in the center of the kitchen, Rina said, "I must admit I'm pretty impressed."

"Don't be too much. I bought the dough from a pizza place across town. It freezes well. And the sauce isn't mine either."

"Hey, you're still doing better than I could. I'm a fair cook—I had to learn or starve to death on the food the General thought edible—but it never occurred to me to make my own pizza."

"Yeah, mess-hall food kills your taste buds. The first thing I did when I got back to the States was eat the biggest, greasiest, juiciest hamburger I could find."

The rapture on his face at the memory made her smile.

"Yeah. For me it would probably be a loaf of homemade bread. I'm such a carb fiend."

"You've certainly earned them tonight. I think you single-handedly painted half the room."

She grunted a skeptical sound but didn't dispute his statement. She had sort of attacked the project with an edge of desperation.

They were almost through with the pizza, one of the best she'd ever eaten, when he looked up from his empty plate. She could tell from the tilt of his head and the intensity in his eyes that he thought she wasn't going to like what he had to say next. Steeling herself, Rina waited.

"You never talk about your mother."

It wasn't a question but she knew what he was asking. Her

mother was a subject she seriously disliked to think about, let alone talk about.

At least she loved her father. And knew he loved her even if he had a difficult time showing it sometimes. Her mother was a whole other kettle of fish.

"She left when I was just shy of five. Couldn't take the military life, the constant moving and isolation." Not to mention her father's high expectations and low threshold for complaints. "She died several years later. A car accident coming home from a late-night shift at the bar."

She didn't mention that it was her mother who'd been the drunk driver. Or that she looked exactly like the woman and had spent the better part of her life trying to live down that fact.

She didn't want to be her mother, selfish, flighty, uncontrolled. The General had raised her to be competent, self-sufficient, to not rely on anyone else for anything. And she'd learned her lesson well because at any moment she could be left all alone. Her mother had chosen to leave. Her father had chosen a career that could make her an orphan.

"I like to think that at some point they loved each other. My father always said they did. I just don't think either of them could handle the pressure of marriage."

"That must have been tough. Growing up without a mother."

"Dad and I managed. Usually without threat of killing each other." Rina smiled, although the effort felt brittle and ready to crack at the first sign of a prodding finger at the open wound. Their relationship was complicated. He'd expected a lot of her and she'd tried hard to live up to the expectations that he had. It was a tough line to walk. But she'd managed.

"Your father never remarried?"

"No. I think he decided dealing with one female was enough. Besides…I think he was afraid to find another woman who couldn't live with him, his lifestyle and his drive for power and success."

"He seems rather single-minded."

Now that was an understatement if ever she'd heard one. "But enough uninteresting details about my childhood." Rina glanced down at her watch. "I should be getting home."

Scraping back her chair from the table, she walked her plate to the dishwasher and loaded it.

"You don't have to do that." Chase's voice sounded directly behind her. She leaned into the counter for a moment, trying to steady her nerves and resolve before turning around.

He was centimeters from her, close enough that she could see the five-o'clock shadow darkening his chin, especially the dimple in the very center, making him look even more rugged and dangerous than usual. It was way past five o'clock. Way past time for her to go.

"Old habits." She attempted a laugh that sounded more like a rush of air escaping from a punctured tire.

With a single step, Chase closed the gap between them. She watched as awareness flared deep in his bright blue eyes, an answering spike of knowledge shooting her body.

He reached for her, running his finger down between her eyebrows, across the bridge of her nose.

"You have tiny dots of paint all over your face."

"I must look like hell."

"Actually, it's rather cute."

"Cute. Every woman's dream."

His fingers grabbed at a tendril of hair brushing gently at her face and ran down the strand. A sharp shiver of need racked her body.

"In your hair, too. *Cute* was the wrong word, but I thought *sexy* would scare the hell out of you."

It did more than that. It made her heart flop over in her chest and her stomach pulse with nervous energy.

"Nothing a shower can't fix." She forced out the words even though her brain was yelling at her to say something else, something along the lines of *take me now.*

His breath pulled sharply into his body; she heard the sound and saw the answering rise of his chest, felt it expand against her as he leaned closer.

Her eyes widened. Had she said that aloud?

His mouth touched down to hers, soft, gentle, persuasive. And she was lost.

Grabbing his face with both hands, she pulled him closer against her body. He went right along with her, deepening the kiss, opening his mouth, raking inside.

His fingers curled into her waist, arching her back and wrapping her tight against him. His body was tense, hard, perfect against her own.

His hands ran up and down her spine for several seconds before he groaned and tore his mouth away, lifted her up by her hips and placed her onto the counter behind them.

Her legs spread out before him, a welcoming V that she couldn't seem to close, didn't want to close. His arm around her back, he scooted her to the very edge so that their bodies aligned perfectly.

A moan escaped from deep in his chest, rumbling with the intensity of a jet overhead. At least, the sound echoed through her the same, jolting, jiggling, tingling inside.

"God, Sabrina, you have no idea how much I want you."

His words played against the curve of her neck, the sensitive spot at the dip of her shoulder. Her skin pebbled, a chain reaction racing down her body.

Her legs wrapped tightly around his waist, needing to pull him closer to her aching core. It was a motion from her memory…from the night of the wedding…this afternoon when he'd teased about having her legs around him. It was a motion that snapped her sanity back into focus.

Pushing him away, Rina slid from the counter onto shaky legs.

"I need to go."

"Don't." Chase reached for her, his lips pinched tight, his eyes swirling with need and disappointment.

She understood. Oh, boy, did she. But that didn't change what she had to do. Her body might be urging her to stay but her brain was yelling at her to leave.

Chase Carden had a control over her she didn't understand. A control that scared her. He was a pilot. Just like her father. He took risks. Unnecessary risks. If she gave in to the urges swirling through her body—the need, that driving force inside—she wasn't sure she'd be able to let him go.

And she wasn't sure she could ever be happy or free of fear if she didn't.

8

"FUNNY. I never took you for a coward before."

Chase lounged inside the doorway of Sabrina's office late Monday morning. She hadn't come to help him paint yesterday. The way she'd left Saturday night like a fire had been lit beneath her butt, he hadn't really expected her to.

However, he'd been disappointed just the same. Saturday had been the first day he'd honest to God enjoyed since coming home.

If there was one thing he knew about his wife it was that calling her out for her evasive tactic was a surefire way to get under her skin. She'd hate being called a coward almost more than anything. Especially because in this case it was true and there was no way she could dispute the fact.

It was an honor thing that her father and the air force had pounded into her brain. He was hoping for a knee-jerk one-eighty reaction that might involve finishing his bedroom…and then making use of it.

"I resent that statement."

"Honey, if it walks like a duck, looks like a duck and quacks like a duck—" he wandered into her space, deliberate rolling steps designed to set her on edge "—then I'm guessing it's a duck."

He enjoyed watching her fluster, the way she tucked a stray strand of hair behind her ear. How her skin flushed a slight shade of pink as he moved closer. The way her body slid against leather as she shifted nervously in her chair.

"What I can't figure out is, are you afraid of me—" Chase leaned down to her ear "—or of yourself?"

She gulped, the elegant column of her throat drawing his gaze down even as her eyes narrowed and her body moved away from him.

"I think you don't trust yourself. I think if you had stayed Saturday night you would have ended up naked on my kitchen counter, relishing every moment of making love with me again."

Chase swiveled her chair around so that she couldn't evade him, couldn't ignore him. She stared up into his eyes, a green swirl of denial, desire and distress.

"And I think you know it."

Sabrina licked her lips before saying, "We agreed we wouldn't do this."

"Yeah, well. I was stupid to think I could be in the same zip code with you and resist craving you."

"Then we can't be in the same zip code, Chase. This is a bad idea. Sleeping together is a bad idea. I've already told you why."

Sleeping together was the wrong term. It was too tame. What they had was raw, unbridled, wild. But he'd keep that thought to himself. For now.

Still, that didn't mean he wasn't going to push her. And if that meant a little personal gratification…

"Hot sex is never a bad idea, Sabrina."

Reaching down, he pulled her out of her chair in one swift motion that had the breath backing into her lungs. Good, he liked her a bit off balance.

"Chase." His gut clenched, not at the sound of his name on her lips but the underlying current of need behind it. She might not realize it but she was begging him—and torturing the hell out of them both.

Reaching into her hair, he grabbed pins, dropping them carelessly on the floor at their feet. He wanted to see the honey-gold mass down, curling around her face and shoulders. He wanted to see the siren she'd been Saturday night in his kitchen, not the damn wall she hid behind at work.

"Why, Sabrina? Why do you hide yourself away? You aren't doing yourself any favors."

"I…I don't. It's regulations."

"I'm not talking about your hair. You're bright, creative, fiery, but I'm apparently the only one who sees that. I'm the *only* one you let see that. Why? What is so wrong with who you really are that no one else can see?"

He stared down into her eyes, bright green, the golden edges pulsing with what she wouldn't let out.

"On our wedding night you didn't fight, you didn't think, you just did what felt right. Why can't you do that now?"

"Because people could get hurt."

"Because *you* could get hurt."

"Yes."

"I won't hurt you, Sabrina."

"You won't mean to but you will." The certainty in her eyes cut him to the core. Just the simple fact that she believed it of him, believed that there was no way their relationship could have a happy ending, no way she could trust in them enough to make it work…

In that moment Chase debated telling her he didn't want the annulment. Would she believe him then? But he took a step back because he knew that's what she wanted.

"We can't ignore each other, Sabrina. And I won't ignore the fact that I want you."

Opening her mouth, she snapped it shut and gazed at him for a moment before saying, "Why not?"

"Because while you don't seem to have a problem lying

to yourself, I'm not willing to do that. Each time I see you, I want you more. It isn't going away, it's getting stronger."

Her eyes widened and her tongue rushed out to lick across her lips. His jaw clenched against the urge to chase it back into her mouth.

"We'll be working together, every day, for the next year. You honestly think you'll be able to keep fighting this?"

"I can go weeks without seeing most of the pilots, at least while we're not touring."

"Yes, but I have no intention of making it that easy for you, Sabrina. You're fighting a losing battle. The sooner you admit that the sooner we'll both be happy...not to mention satisfied."

Sabrina leaned forward, placing her palm to his chest. His heart began to thump with anticipation before he realized she was simply pushing him out of her way.

Stalking across the room, she positioned herself next to the bookshelf...her desk conveniently between them. "I can't do that, Chase. I won't do that."

Of course, she couldn't make things easy. Nothing about Sabrina McAllister was easy. But that was one of the things he enjoyed about her. She certainly offered a challenge. She kept his blood flowing hot and his mind working overtime in order to try and outfox her maneuvers. It was almost as good a high as flying...without the fear of death.

"At least we both know where we stand. You'll change your mind, Sabrina. And when you do...I'm going to enjoy watching you squirm." Now that would be a sight worth fighting for; his wife writhing beneath him, begging for release.

Rina looked up at Chase, imploring him with her eyes to understand. "Please, Chase, I need you to leave me alone. Let me do my job. Let me put this behind me."

DONALD WATCHED the man pull into a parking space in front of his apartment. He couldn't seem to stop himself.

Ever since last week when he'd delivered that note in person, he'd been watching Major Charles Edward Carden.

He'd watched as the man had opened his front door, looked around and seen the note sitting on his front stoop. And part of him had liked the brief flash of surprise, fear and frustration he'd seen in the other man's eyes.

They were the same emotions he'd lived with every day since the casualty notification officer had arrived on his doorstep to tell him that his daughter was dead.

Opening that door, seeing the man standing there silent, somber, in uniform…he'd known. Just as Major Carden had known when he'd seen the note waiting for him.

Still he woke up every morning, forgetting she was gone, expecting for the phone to ring, to hear her voice… Then came the surprise and pain every day when he remembered it hadn't been a bad dream.

The frustration that no one seemed to remember or care about the sacrifice his daughter had made. No, everyone talked about the flyboy, not the woman who'd died so he and the senator could escape unharmed.

And fear. Fear that he'd never find himself again. That until he made things right for his Amy nothing could ever be right.

He'd lost his job with a commercial security firm weeks ago. They'd said they just couldn't keep him on…he'd exhausted his bereavement leave and vacation and wouldn't come back.

Margaret didn't understand. She'd gone on with her life, or was trying to. He didn't blame her. He would have, too…if he could.

He'd stopped calling home. Better she think he chose to stay in the seedy motel room on the outskirts of Las Vegas because he had a gambling problem or had found some hooker. Better for her. At least then he could insulate her from the truth. She didn't need to know their Amy's death had been unnecessary, preventable.

But he wouldn't leave, wouldn't return home to D.C. He wouldn't leave until someone, anyone, *Major Carden* acknowledged his little girl's death.

If that meant spending days lurking around the base so he could watch Carden's every move... If that meant spending nights in his car just so that he wouldn't miss a moment of seeing his baby girl's killer walking open and free in the sunlight...

Then that's what he'd do.

For now.

CHASE SAT DOWN at the bar table across from Jackhammer, waving silently at Sadie as he settled into his chair.

"Find out anything?"

"No. Look, man, I think it's time to tell someone about this."

He'd expected the argument from his friend, they'd had it already.

"And tell them what? We haven't found anything concrete."

"Yeah, well maybe you let someone else, someone whose job it is to investigate this kind of stuff, come to that conclusion."

At first he'd simply been pissed that someone thought they could mess with his life. He'd fought against the increased guilt that the notes and their messages produced inside.

"It's probably just some crackpot antiwar advocate looking to use my story and medal ceremony to make headlines and interrupt the President's schedule."

Jackhammer cocked an eyebrow and stared hard at him.

Yeah, he didn't really think that either. The notes hit too close to home for them not to have some teeth behind them.

"What's the worst that can happen? Someone makes a scene at my award ceremony for the medal I don't want in the first place. There are worse things in this world."

"Something tells me the air force wouldn't exactly jump for joy if that happened, buddy boy. Especially considering you haven't told anyone about this yet. At least if they know they can't blame you for blindsiding them with a PR nightmare starring the President of the United States."

Chase winced. He wanted to take care of this himself. Because whoever was behind it didn't deserve to go to jail…not on top of possibly losing a loved one. The letters had an edge of manic desperation that he could understand. It was why he'd given Jackhammer the short list of army personnel and had taken the list of family members. He really thought it was one of them. He just had to figure out which one.

He wanted to be the one to handle it. It was the least he could do. He owed the dead that.

"Have you told your girlfriend? I bet she'll be pissed if her perfect ceremony gets shanghaied by someone with an embarrassing agenda. You won't be the only one looking like an ass."

And frankly, that was one of his biggest concerns. Whether he wanted her to be or not, Sabrina was in the middle of this.

He just didn't want her in the line of fire of whatever went down. If he went to anyone, she'd be given the information. And she'd consider it her duty to put herself square in the path of any flying punches—real or verbal.

"Give me another couple of days. Long enough to look at all of the families on my list. If I haven't turned up anything then, I'll go to my commander."

He could tell Jackhammer wasn't entirely thrilled with his request.

"I have just over a week before the ceremony."

"Five days, man. If you haven't come up with anything by then I'm reporting it to your commander and I don't care if you like it or not."

"Fair enough."

So for the next five days he'd be busting his butt gathering intelligence. Only one of the families on his list lived close by—in Arizona. He'd maybe take his private plane on a trip that way.

The others would require he spend hours on the Internet and call in a few favors…he'd trade on his current notoriety if he had to.

There were six total—the one in Arizona, two in California, one each in New York, Maryland, and Texas.

He'd eliminate the CA ones first and work his way east.

At least one good thing would come of this—he'd be able to do exactly as Sabrina asked and leave her alone for a few days.

Maybe by then she'd realize it was the last thing she really wanted.

9

THE DAMN MAN had done exactly what she'd asked. And it was driving her bonkers. Rina hadn't seen or heard from him in almost two days.

He hadn't come into her office with that damn knowing smile and his ocean-deep eyes full of mischief. She hadn't seen his face or even heard the deep rumble of his voice.

And she missed it. She missed him.

He crowded her thoughts. She found herself waiting, on edge, for the moment he'd ramble back into her life. Waiting for the moment she'd feel…alive, electrified, free.

She shouldn't want it. Didn't want it. Couldn't help but want it.

Finally, unable to take any more, she headed over to his apartment Friday night. The more she waited, the more she wanted…the less she'd be able to restrain her reaction to him. This way she'd have some control over herself, her emotions. At least that's what she told herself.

But she wouldn't give him the satisfaction of knowing he was right, of knowing she couldn't resist him.

"Have you signed those papers yet?"

Chase had opened his apartment to her, a paint roller in one hand, the door firmly lodged in the other. He stared at her for several moments before finally stepping back and letting her inside.

"Have you?"

"No." Chase turned away.

"What do you mean, no?" Rina couldn't control the physical responses ping-ponging through her body. The reaction was immediate. The moment she'd stepped inside his space, been surrounded by *him,* a craving had settled bone deep.

She'd wanted him to stay away. But she needed this sensation more. The past two days had been stressful, grueling and wearing on her spirit. She'd felt strangled, by her job, her responsibilities, her fear—despite the fact that she'd tried to ignore it—that he'd listen to her and leave her alone. Never in her life had she needed Chase's infusion of passion and confidence more.

He ignored her, walking across the room toward an open door.

"Where are you going?"

He stopped for a split second, not turning around to answer her, instead throwing a response over his shoulder. Holding up the paint roller, he said, "I'd think that would be obvious. I'm going to finish painting."

Saying nothing more, he disappeared into the next room. Rina stood in the middle of his living room, his newly painted living room, and stared after him.

If she went in there she knew exactly what was going to happen. Her, Chase, in a room with a bed—sex would be inevitable. But if she was honest with herself, isn't that why she'd come over here in the first place?

She didn't want to fight it anymore. Didn't want to fight him anymore.

What she did want was the way he made her feel by simply looking at her with those blazing blue eyes, like she was the best thing to happen since frozen pizza dough. What she wanted was the sensation of finally being free, the sensation she only ever experienced when she was with him.

She stopped in the doorway to his bedroom and looked around. The brand-new, huge bed topped with a nice, fluffy mattress sat in the center, draped with plastic. The only other piece in the room was a matching mirror set off toward the corner.

"If you're just here about the papers then why don't you leave? I'm a little busy."

Rina sauntered into the room and, with rolling, purposeful steps, headed straight for him. It was sex. Great sex. But nothing more. It wouldn't change anything. She wouldn't let it.

Leaning up on tiptoe she placed her hand at his waist for balance and whispered, "I have a better idea," against his skin, using his own words against him.

He stilled, paint roller tight in his fist.

"And what would that be?"

Reaching for the roller, she pulled it from his hand. He easily let it go, reaching for her as he turned to face her.

"Painting." Rolling a dark brown stripe down the side of his cheek, Rina couldn't help but laugh at the expression on his face. It was priceless.

And she never, ever, would have followed through on the impulse with anyone else. Somehow she knew no one else in her life would understand. But he would.

Chase grabbed for her wrist, holding tight, not enough to bruise, just enough to keep her from striking again while he wasn't looking. Good thing, too—she wasn't above using diversionary tactics.

Mischief and an answering happiness echoed in his deepening blue eyes, making her heart seem lighter than it had in…a very long time.

She threw back her head and laughed. It felt wonderful.

"You do realize this means war, right?"

HER WRIST IN ONE HAND, Chase watched her laugh. It was an amazing sound, one he'd begun to fear he wouldn't get to hear ever again. She'd finally given in. It was a good thing, too, because he was about on the edge. Every day without seeing her had turned a little more gray.

Glancing down, he saw the paintbrush handle sticking out of a puddle of chocolate paint on the tray at his feet and remembered how adorable she'd looked last weekend with it peppering her honey-blond hair.

Reaching down, he snatched it, dabbed a tiny dot on the end of her nose—or rather what he'd meant to be a tiny dot—and smacked her on the ass.

She yelped and jumped backward, almost plastering herself to the still-wet wall. The gleam of battle entered her eyes, stoking the arousal that streamed ever faster into his blood.

Sabrina would always give as good as she got.

She pried his fingers off of her wrist, twisting from his grasp in one fluid motion. She came up with the roller, but that was fine with him. His brush had distance.

She gave a lightning glance around her, not letting her eyes stray from him for more than a fraction of a second. A mile-wide grin split her face. He knew the moment she spied the pan of paint lying on the floor across the room—her smile got wider. With a coil of muscles, she dashed to the side. He was only a step behind and he probably could have stopped her. But where was the fun in that?

As she reached the second tray, she swooped down, loaded the roller with an almost golden color of paint and swirled to meet him. Crouching into a fighter's pose, she waved the thing in his direction and taunted.

"Come on. I dare you."

He might be a well-trained fighter pilot, but he usually had the aid of million-dollar equipment when he went into battle. Sabrina was a brown belt in karate, or so he'd been told. He hadn't a doubt in his mind that she could take him down.

But it would be a hell of a lot of fun when she did.

He lowered his stance, grounding his body through his center of gravity. He could rush her, but there was the possibility she could really get hurt. Not enjoyable at all. Instead, he waited for her to move, knowing that her patience wouldn't last long. She was a woman of action, always had been and always would be.

After about thirty seconds of watching her, he was rewarded when she charged, and slapped the roller clear down the center of his face.

He heard her giggle but couldn't open his eyes to see her expression.

"Now that's funny." She taunted him, her body close enough for her breath to warm the skin of his back through the cotton of his T-shirt. He sensed her, just by listening to the creak of the floor beneath the shift of her weight on the balls of her feet. Her scent, paint-covered strawberries, eddied and swirled, stronger and lighter as she moved around him—a step back and away, a step forward.

He turned his head to follow her, letting her know he could pinpoint her even with his eyes painted shut. "Says the girl with a chocolate-colored nose. You better check and see if it's cold. Or is it wet? Either way maybe you should see the vet."

She spun around behind him; he could hear the bounce of her feet against the hardwood floor. He was wiping the paint from his eyes when she landed a loud, wet smack to the seat of his jeans.

"Hey!" He jumped forward, almost pitching over.

"That's what you get for smacking my ass. I don't suggest you do it again."

Oh, that was it. Whirling into her next attack, he got a cheekful of paint-covered nap. She hadn't expected him to turn so she'd clocked him good. The spot stung.

And his body ached. For her.

Swatting the roller out of the way, he grabbed for her, pulling her into his already aroused body.

His arms closed around her. It felt so good to hold her again, to know that she belonged to him, and only him. His mouth crushed down to hers, taking from her, forcing her to give.

To his utter amazement, she didn't protest. Instead, she opened for him, her own hands curling into his neck and dragging him closer.

A high-pitched sigh of surrender escaped her lips, cut off before it was fully out by the thrust of his tongue into her mouth.

His hands tore at her clothes, jerking fabric, ripping seams. He didn't care. She could borrow some of his, or stay naked for the rest of their lives.

Her own fingers pushed and pulled, knocking him off balance and sending him sprawling onto the bed he'd moved to the center of the room. Plastic crumpled beneath his back as it stretched and pulled.

"Your new bed."

"I don't care."

"You will when it's covered in paint."

He stared up into her eyes, flashing green rimmed in gold. "No. I won't."

Her hair hung sideways from the clip she'd used to pull it up. Reaching for it, he released the hold, letting the dark blond sheet fall down around them both. It was beautiful and shut out the world. Nothing else mattered but them.

She moved to pull away. He wasn't sure why but he

wouldn't let her go. Not now. Not ever. Sabrina Carden was his.

The vehemence of the thought, almost unrecognizable as his own, surprised him. And scared him. Because he wasn't entirely certain he had the ability to make it true. Sabrina was a strong woman. An independent woman. A woman he could not bend to his will by sheer simple force.

If she was to be his…she'd have to make that decision on her own. And tonight was just one more step in coaxing her there.

Her eyes clouded, desire warring desperately with hesitation.

Chase grasped her hand, pulling her closer to him, tugging her down beside him. She didn't resist. Didn't even put up an effort. Instead, her body landed atop his own, "Oh hell," whooshing from her lungs.

He managed to get out, "Not hell. Heaven," before his lips found hers. He remembered the sensation, had felt it several times since he'd come home. But tonight, it was different. Tonight she was just as she'd been eleven months before, un-inhibited, demanding…alive.

There was no holding back, no second-guessing. She was free and, in letting that part of herself go, she released a hold he hadn't even realized had been over him.

His hands found her body, pulling her close for the sheer unadulterated pleasure of feeling her skin next to his own. He wallowed in the sensation for several moments before pushing her away.

Chase stared down into her face, into her eyes, vibrant, pulsing green. He let his own travel her body, relishing the way her nipples pebbled beneath her shirt at nothing more than the touch of his gaze.

He couldn't stop himself. His hand plunged into the sagging neckline of her shirt. He thrust a hand beneath the satin of her bra to find the silk of her body beneath. Chase cupped her breast, the point there tightening, thrusting, burning a hole at the center of his palm.

"God, you're so responsive." He looked into her eyes, wanting her to know what she could do to him. "It drives me mad. Seeing you every day, buttoned up and pristine, knowing that beneath all the prim and proper lies a sex goddess."

A breath caught in her throat. He could hear the edge of it as it scraped for release. An answering catch jerked in his belly, making him crave.

"I'm no sex goddess."

"Oh, I think you are."

Releasing her, he took several moments to relieve her of the clothes that were left. He cast them aside, uncaring when he heard the liquid plop of paint splattering onto plastic. They were already ripped, what was a little dab of color?

Sabrina stretched before him on his brand-new bed, naked as the day she was born. Beautiful… "Gorgeous."

With slow hands, he ran them up her body. Her skin was pliant and soft, the muscles beneath hard and supple. She let him explore, moving her body, arching her back, thrusting her breast into his hand when he traveled close enough to touch.

He kneaded and tugged, tempted and teased.

His fingers found the center of her body, hot and slick. He played at the folds of her sex, running a finger around the edge, enjoying the feel of her soaked skin and the way her hips arched up to meet him.

Her thighs dropped, open wide for him. She was pink and plump, swollen with a desire that throbbed in time with his own speeding pulse. Bending down, he placed his mouth just there. Her body convulsed with a quick shudder as his tongue laved her, sweeping up to caress the tiny bud of her clit.

He slipped a finger inside her, relishing the way the muscles of her body wrapped around him, coaxing him further in. He lifted his head, wanting to see her face, her eyes glazed dull and sightless with passion…passion for him.

"Chase." The word was no more than a breath. But her eyes, they pleaded with him, deep, dark pools of green.

He wanted nothing more than to sink into her, for it to be over and them both to be satisfied. And it would be good. But they would both miss so much. It could be better.

"Not yet."

Sabrina groaned, a protesting sound that halfway through turned into a growl. Wrapping both of her legs around his thighs, she reached out and grasped his arms. His body twisted with hers, collapsing beneath her.

He heard the sucking sound of plastic as it came away from her damp skin. His senses filled with her scent, sex and strawberries, as he dropped.

She loomed above him, her eyes glowing, a satisfied smile curling her lush lips. With nothing more than a jerk on his shirt, she commanded that he lift up and let her take it from him.

Her deft fingers unbuttoned the fly of his jeans. The bite of the zipper and the heat of her touch brushed down his aching erection. She didn't touch skin on skin, instead making sure to torment him even more than he'd teased her.

Dragging herself up from the bed, she stood at the edge of the mattress, a fisted hand tugging at the cuff of each leg until his pants fell to the floor. He hadn't bothered with anything underneath…he hadn't exactly expected it to matter.

Her grin widened as she gazed down at him. He enjoyed the way her eyes dilated, enjoyed knowing she gained pleasure from looking at his body.

"Pretty gorgeous yourself."

With a laugh, he raised his arms and pillowed them beneath his head. "I do my best."

Shaking her head, Sabrina climbed onto the bed, kneeling between his legs. His breath caught at the picture of her there, knowing her mouth, her hands were so close. She could give him unbelievable pleasure. The image of her mouth, slick, wet, a dot of white frosting at the edge, swam across his mind. Had given him unbelievable pleasure.

Her palms slapped down onto his chest. The tops of her thighs brushed his own. Her body planked out above him, only touching him palm to chest and thigh to thigh.

His cock strained between them, jerking towards her as she rocked her body gently above him.

"We seriously need to do something about that ego."

"My ego's fine. But there are certainly other parts of me that could use some attention."

She laughed, her head thrown back, the sound erupting from deep in her belly. When she leaned forward again, a single curl of her hair slipped from her back, falling down to tickle the center of his chest.

The caress was light, too light. He wanted more of her. Grasping her hips, he jerked her off center, her elbows buckling beneath her. Their bodies collided, skin on skin. It was the best sensation he'd experienced for months.

Unable to stop an unexpected surge of emotion, Chase wrapped his fingers tightly around her hips. He knew he was hurting her, could see her wince of pain. But he couldn't make his hands relinquish her. For a split second he was utterly terrified that if he let go, even an inch, she would disappear. And never come back.

That he would lose the one thing that was keeping him centered right now.

Closing his eyes for a moment, he willed the thought away. Sabrina wasn't going anywhere. At least not tonight. His hold relaxed and he inhaled her scent. He relished the feel of her body against his own and simply enjoyed.

But he didn't stay that way long. The fire bursting through his blood wouldn't allow him that. It demanded respite, release.

He slipped a hand between their bodies, finding the core of her hot and wet. A single finger inside had the breath surging from her lungs, tickling a path across his face. She rocked against him, a mindless, increasing rhythm that told him everything he needed to know.

She whimpered as he released her.

"Soon, baby, soon," he soothed as he grasped her hips and slid home deep inside her.

The plastic was sticky and stiff under his body. It had slipped and bunched in places. He didn't care. The only thing that mattered was Sabrina, the glove-tight hold she had around his body.

She sat up, her nails digging crescents into his chest as she fought for a grip. Her eyes struggled to half-mast but she wouldn't let them close all the way. Instead, her gaze locked with his as she rocked her hips back and forth against his body.

She sucked him in, her breasts swaying seductively, calling to him. Rearing up, he took one tight, pink bud into his mouth, sucking hard before laving it with his tongue. He loved the sensation of her pebbled skin, the tear of electricity that shot through his body at the touch.

She reached behind her, changing the angle of her body, forcing him higher and harder inside her. Her palm landed on the outside of his thigh, and he felt the brush of it and heard the rustle of plastic.

Her body tightened around him. A keening moan rumbled

from between her parted lips. And all the while she watched him with hot, burning eyes.

Her mouth opened on a silent cry that finally burst free as her body contorted with the force of her orgasm. Her muscles contracted around and above him.

It was an amazing sight, one he wasn't likely to ever forget as long as he lived. Her hair rolling free and tangled down her back. Her body glowing with the sheen of sweat and pleasure. Open and uninhibited, for him, only for him.

That realization burst through him, vaulting him to a heart-stopping release of his own. He pumped high and hard inside as Sabrina rocked along with him, milking his body and pulling the last possible moments of ecstasy from the experience.

Minutes later she collapsed beside him, half on and half off his body, and mumbled, "The plastic's got to go."

Her face was buried between his ribs and his arm. Her breath tickled against his skin, leveling eventually to something approaching normal.

One arm wrapped tightly around her waist, he relished the moment, enjoying the feel of simply holding her next to him.

Until she ruined it.

"You do know we need to keep this to ourselves right? A one-time thing that shouldn't get in the way of our annulment. And definitely shouldn't happen again."

Her body stiffened against him as she waited for his response. Tension snapped through her yet again. Why couldn't she just relax? Enjoy.

Chase sighed. The feeling of contentment had lasted roughly three minutes. He supposed he should be grateful for that. But he couldn't lie to her. Not now. Not after what they'd just shared.

"I don't want an annulment."

10

"WHAT THE HELL do you mean you don't want an annulment?"

Rina shoved up from the bed, using his chest as leverage to get herself away. And it was a good thing, too, because she was starting to feel altogether too comfortable in his arms.

She could get used to that sensation. And that would not be good. She was scared. Scared that with one unbelievably reckless and amazing moment she'd tied herself irrevocably to this man, to this pilot, to this idiotic hero.

"Well, considering what just happened, I don't think an annulment is an option anymore."

"Shit!"

Chase simply shrugged—the damn man—and smiled at her. The sort of smile that said he'd won a battle she hadn't even been aware they'd been fighting.

Oh, she'd known he'd wanted sex. If she was honest with herself, she'd admit that she'd wanted it as well. But *her* willpower had been stronger than the urges.

Or so she'd thought. So much for mind over matter.

"Honestly, Sabrina. I don't see the problem."

"Obviously. That doesn't mean it isn't there."

She'd spent the past weeks of her life planning a medal ceremony for the night he'd almost died. Every day he went up in that plane was a day an accident might happen, a day he might not come back. The man took risks. Risks her damn heart couldn't stand.

Not to mention the small fact that they could both lose their positions with the squadron, receive a formal reprimand that would tank their careers or possibly be court-martialed for fraud if anyone found out about their marriage.

And if the air force found out, her father would. And he wouldn't be able to keep his nose out of it. He'd ride in like some knight in shining armor and try to protect her…no matter if she wanted the protection or not.

He'd be mad she hadn't told him, upset that she'd done something so stupid to ruin her career…and he'd be right, damn it.

She'd had a plan. But with Chase, her plans seem to melt away. Instead, the wild child she'd been ignoring since she was five took over.

Rina groaned. "We go through with the annulment." It was the best thing for them both even if he didn't realize it yet.

Chase reached for her. She twisted out of his grasp, walking away toward the window. But he followed her, wrapping his arms around her waist and neatly blocking off all of her exits.

The warmth of his body burned into her back. His arms were red-hot bands around her stomach. And her skin felt itchy and tight. Her head told her to run away. But her body refused to listen.

"Look, that option is gone. Although, I can't say I'm terribly upset."

"What?" What was wrong with him? "We don't even know each other, Chase. Just because we said 'I do'—without realizing it was for real, I might add—doesn't mean we should stay married. In fact, it means we should end it as soon as possible. We don't belong together."

"You're wrong." His mouth nuzzled at her neck, sending a thrill of awareness down her spine. "We certainly have sexual chemistry."

Her chest tightened at the shot of pleasure spilling into her veins. She needed to get away from him. Right now. Because if she didn't she was afraid she'd never have the strength to step away.

He had the huge potential to break her heart. The Babe Magnet would get tired of her...that's what he did. He'd move on—other women, other assignments, more dangerous stunts, more heroic maneuvers.

Her parents' marriage had started out as an instant attraction, love at first sight, her father had told her. And look how well that had turned out. Attraction always faded away. And where would they—she—be when it did?

She couldn't stay here. She couldn't risk that. It was cleaner, safer her way.

Lifting her foot, Sabrina stomped squarely on his instep. Chase's grunt of surprise and pain whooshed past her ear, tickling the tender shell and sending another unwanted shiver through her body.

His arms dropped away, leaving her naked, alone and somehow disappointed. She ignored the sensation.

Turning toward him, she said, "You're delusional, Chase. There is no us. There never has been and there never will be. A relationship—a marriage—takes a hell of a lot more than sexual chemistry to make it work. It isn't a mistake you make and decide to keep just because the sex is great. It's something you dream about for years, something you plan."

He rubbed at the center of his foot, hopping up and down. She fought against a laugh and the urge to reach out and grab him. On one hand it was somewhat comical, the way the moonlight fell across his naked, contorted body. On the other, unfortunately arousing.

"Plan. Everything in life isn't neat, Sabrina. Everything doesn't fall into line with a plan."

"It does in mine, mister, and I have no intention of making a small mistake bigger because I let idiotic impulses rule my brain."

A flash of something she didn't like crossed his face. It wasn't pain…it couldn't be. She couldn't have hurt him. Not really. It was pride, that was all.

"Besides, all we do is argue."

"That's not true." He gave her a pointed, steamy look that had her insides melting yet again, damn the man. "Of course, we wouldn't argue as much if you'd just admit that you want me."

"Oh, I want you all right. I want you to sign the annulment papers so all this can go away."

"I can't do that. One, I don't want to. And two, I'm not going to lie to the judge. We have a relationship, Sabrina. Even if you'd like to pretend that we don't."

With a growl of frustration, she yanked on her clothes, uncaring that they were covered with drips of paint.

"Fine. I'll call my lawyer tomorrow and rest assured, I'll let you know what he says about divorce."

"ARE YOU GOING to talk to me?"

"Yes."

"About anything important?"

Sabrina looked across her office at Chase as he stood watching her. She wasn't entirely happy to see him this morning, not after the night they'd shared, the night she couldn't seem to put out of her mind no matter how hard she tried. She'd completely forgotten the interviews she'd scheduled for today and the fact that they were supposed to travel into the city together.

She sighed. It had been difficult this morning, putting on her uniform, the layers of armor she used to keep her life ordered and perfect. She hadn't wanted to, but she'd done it anyway.

"Are you ready to go?"

He was here a little early, but better they get things started than stare at each other for the next half hour.

"No."

Grabbing an office chair she'd stashed in the corner, Chase turned away from her and wedged it beneath the handle of the door he'd closed when he'd walked in.

"What are you doing?"

Instead of answering her, he walked across the room. His eyes burned into her body, setting off a chain reaction of sensations. How could he do that? Turn her on with little more than the glitter of promise in his eyes?

"You know, I'm getting really tired of having to convince you this is real, Sabrina. I'm not sure how much longer I can do it. You sure as hell aren't making it easy."

Yeah, well, that wasn't her intention. "Excuse me for trying to be realistic."

"Excuse you for being scared. Fine, I get it."

"Probably not." There was no way he could when even she didn't understand the level of terror that filled her—both at the thought of losing him and at the thought of keeping him in her life.

Reaching for her, he buried his fingers into the hair pulled tight at her nape. The tug hurt a little but, as he leaned down toward her, she decided she didn't care.

"Sabrina, this is real and I'm not going anywhere."

"What are you doing?"

She should stop him.

"Trying to kiss my wife."

"Well, stop."

He stared down at her, frank appreciation stamped on his

face. It was an unsettling and heady sensation, like she was the Christmas present he'd waited all year to open.

"If someone sees us…" Her voice trailed off on the protest she didn't really want to make, not with his fingers trailing slowly and tantalizingly across the front of her shirt. She wanted his touch. Ached for his touch.

"I know. Public displays of affection. Why do you think I stuck a chair under the door?"

"You should still stop." His fingers brushed against the swell of her breast. She instinctively leaned into his hand.

"You don't want me to."

He pulled back, his gaze snagging hers, waiting, demanding she admit to the truth.

And she couldn't give it to him.

She pushed away from her desk and stood up. "We have to go. Move the chair."

DONALD FOLLOWED discreetly behind as the vehicle turned into the parking lot at the *Las Vegas Review Journal.* He'd been surprised to see Carden's car pulling off of the base so early in the day. He'd been there less than an hour.

He wondered who the woman in the car was. She was probably air force since she'd already been on base. He'd love to see her uniform, to figure out what her rank and possible position was.

He drove slowly down the opposite parking aisle, watching and waiting…for what he wasn't sure. A sign. Maybe his Amy would give him one, show him what he was supposed to do.

Pulling around the corner, Donald headed down the same aisle Carden had parked about halfway down. The major was getting out of his car.

It was almost as if time slowed, a perfect storm of meticulous details that fell precisely into place.

Carden walked into the open lot, his attention focused on the car behind him, on the woman staring down into the center console of the car, maybe grabbing something.

He wasn't paying attention. And he was simply there, in front of him, lined up with the hood of his car.

Without thinking, Donald pressed harder on the gas. His car jerked forward at the unexpected rush of fuel into the lines.

The thud was loud in his ears, along with the curse that rang out, echoed back and forth against the closed windows of his car.

Their eyes locked through the windshield and all he could do was stare. He was unable to look away from the man who looked back.

"Chase." It was screamed out into the deathly silence that had descended, breaking the spell wrapped around him.

Donald accelerated as the woman scrambled from the car. He watched in the rearview mirror as she raced up to Carden, who was leaning heavily against the bumper of his car.

She turned her head in his direction, yelling something he could no longer hear.

It didn't matter.

He'd failed. Failed Amy again.

GODDAMN IT! She'd been in control for a full thirty minutes before it had all gone to shit.

Chase could have been killed. Her hands still shook at the memory.

Of course, not as far as he was concerned, stubborn man.

The idiot had actually insisted on going inside and doing the interview she'd scheduled. And he'd refused to limp once they'd gotten around anyone else. No one would have known by looking at him that he'd almost been run over by a car in the parking lot.

She, on the other hand, had been a total basket case. Not her normal comfort zone. In fact, she rather hated it...and him at the moment for making her act that way.

He wouldn't even allow her to look at it, let alone take an aspirin.

Oh, buddy, but he'd be doing both now.

She watched as he limped slightly up the walkway to his apartment. At least he'd listened to her when she'd said she was calling their commander if he didn't take the rest of the day off. Maybe once he was settled she'd convince him that calling the police was a good idea.

"I can't believe that jerk just drove away. Or that you won't let me call anyone."

"I'm fine, Sabrina. And considering we were in the *Journal*'s parking lot, calling in the cops would have started a huge sensation. I can just see the headlines, War Hero Assaulted in Parking-Lot Hit-and-Run. Not exactly great publicity."

"Haven't you ever heard that any publicity is good publicity?"

"Tell that to the air force. I'm fine, Sabrina."

Chase turned around to look at her, a cocky half grin curling at the edges of his lips. That, more than any protest or excuse he'd made in the past few hours, set her nerves a little closer to normal.

"Drop 'em, buddy."

His eyebrows rose practically to his hairline but the grin stayed firmly in place. "Yes, ma'am."

She frowned at him and cocked an eyebrow of her own. Shaking her head, she turned into the kitchen, opened the freezer and found what she was looking for in the back.

The sharp hiss of breath through his teeth made her look over at him. She wasn't exactly happy with what she saw. A nasty bruise about the size of a softball, already purple and yellow in places, covered the side of his thigh. The edges disappeared into the bottom hem of his boxer briefs. She tried not to let her eyes dwell on what else they covered. Now was not the time.

As she watched he poked a finger at it and hissed again. Men.

"Stop that, you idiot. I knew we should have gone to the emergency room."

"It's just a bruise. The guy was barely going five miles an hour. It smarts but it isn't life threatening. I've had worse. I'll live."

Maybe, but for a second she could picture him lying bloody and broken beneath the front tire of that car and had to fight back a shudder.

He watched her with his normal intensity, a sensation she was finally starting to get used to. Not immune to—even underneath the layer of concern for him she couldn't help the awareness.

"The strong will stand, the weak will fall by the wayside."

Rina just rolled her eyes. "Yeah, yeah. I get it. Big strong man can take on a car and win. Now sit your ass down and put these peas on that bruise before I put another one on your skull."

She tossed them to him, not trusting that she wouldn't let the worry and fear get the best of her if she came close enough to get her hands on him. Crying on his shoulder now wouldn't do any good.

He sank down onto the couch letting out a groan of pain that had her shooting forward. He leaned back across the length of the cushions, gingerly placing the frozen veggies on the spot on his thigh.

Through half-closed eyes he watched her.

"You know, now that I think about it there is something you could do."

"Oh yeah, what's that?"

"Kiss it and make it better."

She picked up the first thing that was handy, a flying magazine lying on the coffee table, and chucked it at his head. He reached up, without even opening his eyes all the way, and snatched it out of the air.

"Nice throw."

She grabbed for the stray strands of hair that had fallen from her knot and smoothed them back into place. Smoothing at imaginary wrinkles in the tail of her uniform shirt, she said, "I'm going to check in at the office. Keep your ass on that couch if you know what's good for you."

CHASE WATCHED Sabrina walk into his home office and finally let his head fall back against the arm of the sofa. His thigh throbbed like a son of a bitch but he wasn't about to let her know that. She was jittery enough about the whole thing as it was.

He wasn't an idiot, as much as she seemed to enjoy calling him one—if his injury had been serious he would have gone to the doctor.

He would heal.

The problem was he wasn't entirely certain it wouldn't happen again. He'd gotten a good look at the man behind the wheel. He hadn't been a teenager. He hadn't been drunk. However, he had had blood in his eyes.

The man had been out for revenge…for what, Chase could only guess, but it was a pretty educated one.

The problem was he still had no clue who the man could be. He needed to step up his investigation into the families.

He'd already eliminated the two from California and one from Texas.

He'd lie here for a little while—long enough to convince

Sabrina he was taking it easy—and then fly to Arizona later this afternoon. In the meantime, he wondered if he could convince her of the healing properties of sex.

"What the hell is this?"

At the sound of her voice, her cold and frosty, upset voice, Chase craned his neck around to the doorway.

His heart stuttered and threatened to stop when he looked at what she held in her hand. He didn't need to read them to know it was the white note cards.

Damn! He'd forgotten they were lying on his desk.

"Uh, nothing?"

Yeah, even he wasn't buying that one. But at least it gave him a moment to recover from the shock and swing his feet around to the floor so he could actually face her.

"Try again." The words came through gritted teeth. Oh, she was not happy.

With a sigh, Chase said, "Come here."

"I don't think so."

Holding out his hand, he motioned for her, staring her down and giving her a silent choice. She could leave without getting any more information from him or she could sit down next to him...close enough that he could grab her and talk some sense into her if she decided later that leaving had been the better choice.

With a growl she said, "Fine. But keep your hands to yourself."

He didn't answer. At least this way he wouldn't have to lie to her...although she might think he'd already done that.

She sat down on the couch beside him, then moved as far into the opposite corner as she could get. "Now spill it."

"They started arriving right after I got here."

"How many?"

"Just the two so far." He chopped his words off.

"But…"

Apparently she'd heard the mental pause in his head.

"But nothing."

She stared at him for several minutes. "But you think maybe that was who hit you this morning? Oh, my God, Chase. You really are an idiot. I'm calling the police."

He stilled her forward motion with a hand across her waist.

"Don't."

"Give me one good reason why not."

"Because I'm handling it."

"Oh, you are, are you? That bruise says you're handling it really well."

His hand tightened around the curve of her body, hoping he could make her understand. If anyone would, maybe it would be her.

"I think it's a family member of one of the soldiers we lost that night, Sabrina. I don't want to make things any worse for them."

Her teeth ground together as she stared at him with fear- and anger-filled eyes.

"So instead you're just going to let whoever it is kill you? Maybe next time they won't be going five miles an hour."

"That was an accident, Sabrina. A spur-of-the-moment decision."

"Great, so next time he'll be better prepared. I assume you got a good look at whoever this is?"

"Yes, but I don't know which family he belongs to. I've eliminated a couple already. Jackhammer's been helping me."

"Remind me to yell at him the next time I see him."

Chase grinned. He couldn't help it. She was so fierce and cute when she was upset.

"Look, I've done enough damage to this family, Sabrina. I refuse to do more. All I need is a couple days to sort this out. I've promised Jackson that if I don't have more information by Monday I'll tell the commander."

"Monday."

"Yes."

"What are you planning to do this weekend?"

"I'm flying to Arizona this afternoon."

He watched as her face went pale, every last drop of blood draining away.

"Sabrina? Are you okay?"

"Are you sure you're up to flying?"

"I told you, I'm fine."

"Then I guess I'm coming with you."

PULLING OUT into traffic, Chase headed toward the private airstrip where he housed his plane, an older model Cessna he'd bought sight unseen several months before coming home. He hadn't been disappointed.

While flying jets gave him an adrenaline rush unlike any other, he'd needed something smaller, safer, after months of living on the edge of danger with lives hanging in the balance.

Fifteen minutes later, he parked in front of the hangar. He'd called ahead to have his plane fueled and waiting for them.

He glanced over at Sabrina. She looked…angry. Her jaw was clenched tight enough that he was afraid she was going to throw a filling. Her eyes were trained squarely on the plane sitting across the tarmac before them, narrowed, almost as if she was daring it to—what?—explode?

And then he realized what had her so upset. She didn't want to fly. With *him*. And that stung.

"You know, you don't have to go if you don't want to." His words came out clipped and sharper than he'd intended.

"I'm going." She didn't even turn to look at him, just continued to stare straight ahead.

"Fine. I'm going to do a preflight check before we take off."

It hurt that she didn't trust him. Didn't trust his abilities. He went through his safety inspection, building a nice head of steam while he was at it. When he returned to the car to find Sabrina leaning against the hood, watching him instead of his plane, he couldn't hold back.

"If you don't feel safe in my plane then do us both a favor and stay on the ground."

She turned startled eyes to him.

"What do you mean?"

"I mean, if you don't trust me as a pilot then stay out of my plane. I can tell just by looking that you don't want to go."

Sabrina stared up at him for several seconds. He watched her take a deep breath, the muscles in her face and body relaxing in a slow wave.

"I have no problem with your flying abilities, Chase. I'd trust you with my life." Turning away, she reached inside the car and grabbed her purse. His plan was to come back tonight as soon as he'd talked to the family. He'd briefly flashed on the idea of staying over and taking advantage of having her as a captive audience but had changed his mind. Sabrina wasn't exactly in a receptive frame of mind.

"So, where are we going?"

Pulling her body straight, she hitched the strap up onto her arm, her eyes returning to the plane over his right shoulder. At least her face had lost the pinched, angry look.

"First I thought you'd enjoy seeing the Grand Canyon from the air. Then we'll head to Flagstaff, talk to the family, maybe stop at a nice little place I know for dinner."

"I take it you've already filed a flight plan?"

"Yep."
"Great."
"Great."

11

SHE'D MISCALCULATED. Terribly.

Being ten-thousand feet in the air was bad enough, but gazing down into the biggest gaping hole in North America had her stomach lurching up uncomfortably close to her throat.

It had been eighteen years since she'd gotten airsick, thanks mostly to the wonderful invention of Dramamine and the fact that these days she limited her flying exposure to megalithic monstrosities like C-130s and C-141s.

A four-seater Cessna was a little too small for comfort. There was no escaping the vastness of air and space around her. It stretched out forever in front of her eyes, which she promptly had to close or risk losing the sandwich she'd eaten for lunch. At the moment, she wished she'd skipped it altogether.

"Are you okay?"

She wanted to shake her head but even that movement could dislodge the tight grip she had on her body. If she let go, even a centimeter, it would be all over.

She remembered this, the fervent prayer and hope that she could hold on...just a little bit longer. The last time she'd subjected herself to the torture had been the one and only time her father had coerced her into flying with him.

He'd been so angry with her. She'd been eleven and wanted so badly to please him. The General had insisted it was simply mind over matter and she had nothing to fear.

Instead, she'd thrown up the diner pancakes he'd treated her to, all over his lap. It hadn't even been a jet. No tricks. No Gs. Just a regular old plane that he'd borrowed from a buddy.

He had not been happy.

He'd wanted to show her that there was nothing to fear, being in the air. Instead, he'd unknowingly reinforced her fears. She still didn't like flying; it scared the shit out of her. For the most part she'd developed some coping mechanisms she used when it was unavoidable—like whenever they traveled to shows. She sat where she couldn't see out of the plane and pretended they were just in a really big, really badly sprung car. And took the fully loaded Dramamine that knocked her out.

Unfortunately, she couldn't pretend in this teeny, tiny machine. And the flight hadn't been long enough for the Dramamine, not if she'd wanted to be coherent when they touched ground.

She'd never forgotten the wretched feeling of disappointing her father. Of knowing something he prided himself on, something he enjoyed, made her sick as a dog. It was simply one more thing they couldn't share. More distance in their relationship they couldn't bridge.

They'd never discussed her…failure. Although she knew without a doubt that up until that day it had been her father's wish that she follow in his footsteps and become a pilot just like him.

She didn't like to admit weakness of any sort…to anyone. But talking about her airsickness…it was rather embarrassing considering she served her country in the air force. No one knew. And she wanted to keep it that way.

The thought of losing it in front of Chase left her clammy with sweat, not to mention mortified. She didn't want to disappoint him, too.

"Sabrina. *What's wrong?*"

Leaning her head back against the seat, she breathed slowly through her nose and out her mouth. Big, calming, drafts of air in. Lingering, even streams of air out.

It didn't help.

"Here."

Chase thrust a brown paper bag into her hands. She had no idea where it had come from but at the moment she seriously didn't care.

She grappled for another minute for control only to realize it was a lost cause. Tears pricked at the back of her eyes as she fought the unbelievable feeling of disappointment—in herself and in the realization that she was about to lose a few notches in Chase's opinion of her. It bothered her more than it should.

A minute later it no longer mattered.

"WHY DIDN'T YOU tell me you get airsick?"

Chase sat inside the cockpit of his plane, his body tense, although the trip was finally over.

As much as it had felt like an emergency, watching Sabrina so miserable and uncomfortable, somehow he didn't think the FAA would consider airsickness as dire as, say, a malfunctioning engine.

He'd continued on to Flagstaff, not all that far away. But it had been the longest minutes of his life. By the time they landed, Sabrina's skin was as pale as the snow-white clouds staring down at them.

It scared him to death. And called up an urge to wrap her in his arms and simply never let her go. To keep her safe and protected. No one in his life had ever needed him that way.

"Because I haven't gotten sick in almost eighteen years." She turned watery, miserable eyes towards him. "Since I discovered Dramamine."

"Why the hell didn't you tell me you needed it?"

As he watched, her skin flushed warm, a tide of red rushing up into her neck and face. At least she had some color now.

Her lips clamped shut, thinning to an unbelievably straight line.

Little idiot. Shaking his head, Chase said, "Fine. Don't tell me. But, for heaven's sake, we're stopping at a pharmacy before we head home."

At that her body went pale again. He could see tiny drops of sweat dotting her forehead just at the line of her hair.

"Not now. In fact, I think maybe we'll stay here tonight. Let your stomach settle a bit before we try this again."

That didn't seem to steady her nerves any.

She could not take another flight right now. What she needed was to rest. Luckily, he knew just the place.

He'd been coming here for years. His father, the few times he'd seen the man, had talked to him about how beautiful Arizona was. How peaceful. Being so close, Chase had wanted to experience that peace for himself.

And he'd discovered his father was right. Flagstaff was an interesting town, a mix of hippie and new age. Close enough to the Grand Canyon that he could lose himself in a few days of hiking and camping.

One of the reasons he'd bought the plane before coming home was because he knew he'd need to find that sense of peace again.

To his amazement and consternation, it had eluded him the first time he'd returned. Chase had simply chalked it up to the overwhelming guilt he was still feeling. His mind wasn't ready for peace. But it hadn't been there a few weeks ago when he'd returned again. Then, he'd fought down a minor sense of panic.

"Let's find you someplace you can lie down."

"That would be great."

The grateful look she sent him had his stomach kicking into his chest. Not because he enjoyed the feeling of being needed by her—although he did—but because if she was willing to put aside her all-fired self-reliance and let him take care of her she must be feeling truly awful. Chase didn't like that thought at all.

Sabrina was one of the strongest, most independent women he'd ever met. Seeing her brought so low was…wrong.

He settled her into their waiting rental car. He'd asked for a fire-engine red convertible so that they could put the top down and enjoy the Arizona sun. Instead, she buckled into her seat, rolled her head against the headrest and stared listlessly out the window.

It was early afternoon when he finally got her settled into a hotel room. It was a small place, not part of a large chain, but a tasteful, expensive resort with panoramic views. Relaxing. At least he'd always thought so. Once she rested, he fully expected Sabrina would fall in love with the place as much as he had.

He watched her stretch out on the bed.

"Do you need anything?" Chase walked to her, staring down into her face as she looked up into his. Her skin had gained some color back. But her eyes were still miserable…hurt.

She shook her head.

"Get some rest. You'll feel better."

"What are you doing?"

"I thought I might go into town."

"Don't you dare visit that family without me. Someone already tried to kill you. It's too dangerous."

He nodded simply, agreeing with her that it was dangerous but knowing she'd take it for agreement with her order. However, he wasn't going to waste precious time.

Chase waited for Sabrina's body, exhausted and sick, to pull her into a calming, restoring sleep. And then he left.

The address was easy to find. He sat in the rental car for several minutes staring at the house. He watched as a man—clearly not the one who'd hit him in the parking lot—puttered in the yard in front of the house.

It obviously wasn't them. So why wasn't he leaving?

Maybe because he couldn't sit here, staring at someone who'd been affected by the decision he'd made, and not do something. Say something. The guilt he lived with wouldn't let him.

Getting out, he walked slowly across the street, unsure of what he was going to say. What could he say that would make a difference? Was he doing this for them, or for himself?

The man, Mr. Nesmith according to the information he had, asked, "Can I help you?"

"I'm Major Chase Carden."

"Yes, sir. I know who you are. Nicky watched you on *Oprah*. We appreciated what you said about our boy Max."

Part of him was surprised when the man offered his hand.

"I, ah, was close by and wanted to make sure you'd gotten the invitation to the medal ceremony."

"We did. Thank you for including us. We weren't planning to come, though—it's a little far away for us."

"I don't really deserve the medal and I want to make sure the six that lost their lives that night get the recognition they deserve."

Chase had no idea why he was telling this to a complete and total stranger. Maybe it was his kind face. His understanding eyes. Maybe Chase just needed to tell someone, anyone, connected to the families that he knew he shouldn't be the one getting the attention…their loved ones should.

"Son, I think you do deserve that medal. I think every last

soldier over there deserves a medal for what they do every day. Not everyone gets one. That doesn't mean you shouldn't take yours."

The man looked up at him, shifting on his feet for a second before clapping him on the back.

"What happened isn't your fault. You know that, right? It was war. Max Junior knew what he was signing up for when he decided to go into the army, just like every other soldier. He was prepared to make the ultimate sacrifice for his country if necessary. I won't say it isn't hard, because every day I want him home, safe, back with us. But what happened isn't your fault."

Chase simply nodded, not sure what else to do or say.

"Thank you, sir. If you change your mind about coming, please contact the Thunderbirds public affairs officer. We'll make sure you can get to the ceremony."

Chase started to leave but the other man stopped him.

"Major Carden." Pausing, he looked back. "I might not think you're responsible, but I do know someone who does. I wouldn't be mentioning this except for…well, Nicky's been in touch with his wife and she hasn't seen or heard from him in weeks. She's getting very worried."

"Who is it, sir?"

"Donald Blankenship. His daughter, Amy I think, was in the same platoon with Max. That's how Nicky and his wife met. They have an online support group for family. He needed someone to blame. I guess he's fixated on you."

Chase let the words soak into his skin. It wasn't far off from what he'd expected. That didn't make it any easier to hear.

"Thank you, sir."

Chase headed back to his car, the other man's final words following him. "He's wrong."

Chase wasn't so sure about that.

He drove to the hotel in silence, his mind racing. He hadn't settled on anything, let alone what to do with the information he'd just received by the time he walked back into their room.

He stopped inside the doorway, staring down at Sabrina as she lay sleeping on the bed. Peaceful. Perfect. He couldn't tell her. She'd go straight to the commander, the Secret Service, anyone who could find the man and put a stop to him.

But Chase didn't want that—a swarm of people with guns making the situation worse. Maybe if he could just find the man and talk to him… He'd check the hotels as soon as they got home. If he found nothing then he'd turn the information over.

His gaze followed the softened planes of Sabrina's sleeping face. She was the best thing in his life right now. Nothing else mattered. She was his wife and he never wanted to let her go.

Without thinking, he reached for her, softly trailing a finger down her cheek, brushing a hand across her forehead, moving a few stray strands of her silky hair out of her way.

Her eyes fluttered open. He hadn't meant to wake her. He'd just needed to touch her.

"Hi." The word was sleepy and low, but the smile on her face made his heart ache.

"Feeling better?"

She nodded, sleep letting go slowly of her brain, her body. "Thank you."

"For what?"

She stared up at him for several moments. "For understanding."

"What's there to understand? It isn't like you did anything wrong, Sabrina. This isn't your fault." The strange echo of the words Mr. Nesmith had spoken not twenty minutes before wasn't lost on him.

She scoffed, just as he had to himself. She was wrong. Was he?

"That isn't how my father saw it."

"What does he have to do with this?"

"Nothing."

Picking her up as if she were no more substantial than air, he sat down on the bed, his back braced against the headboard, her head cradled in his lap.

"Tell me."

She sighed, tension stiffening her body before she went lax and pliant against him again. "The General had sole responsibility for me from the time I was five whether he wanted it or not. Worrying about which school I'd go to, what we'd eat for dinner…it wasn't exactly how he'd envisioned his life. And it didn't fit well with his career ambitions. The General never understood how he could have ended up with a daughter…no less a daughter with motion sickness. The only thing he ever wanted was a son to carry on his name, to carry on his legacy within the air force."

"I think you're doing a hell of a job with that, Y chromosome not required."

She shrugged, her shoulders lifting and falling against his thigh. He tried to ignore the sensation; this was not the time to be turned on.

"Sure. But I'm not a pilot and I never could be."

She remained silent for several minutes. He wondered what she was thinking but didn't want to risk asking her. It was the most she'd shared of herself with him in…well, ever. He didn't want to ruin the moment.

"I think somehow he blamed me for his lost dream, his lost legacy. And my mom. He blamed her for a lot of things, although, he had every reason to."

"Now, that's hardly fair."

Her head stirred in his lap. "Do you know exactly how she died?" Her voice was soft…and bleak.

"No."

"She died in a car accident. Drunk. She killed a father and his son. My mother destroyed herself, my family, and two innocent people. She was selfish and hedonistic. She didn't care who she hurt as long as what she did felt good."

Chase wasn't sure what to say to that. Were there words? Instead, he simply placed a hand on her back and caressed up and down.

It told him a lot though, a lot about her, about why she'd resisted giving in to the attraction between them. Maybe now he'd figure out how to keep her with him, knowing why she fought so hard to get free. It was something they shared—a messy divorce and the loss of a parent. Maybe knowing that would help him understand—give him another weapon in his arsenal to fight for her.

"I look like her, you know. My hair. My eyes. I think the only thing I got from the General is his unwavering sense of right and wrong."

"Oh, I think you got a few other things. His confidence. Strength. Stubbornness." He brushed his lips against her forehead.

She laughed, a gentle burst of air that heated the denim beneath her cheek, and the prickling skin beneath.

"He sees her, whenever he looks at me."

"I doubt that. You aren't like her, you know. Even if you let that inner wild child out more often, you still wouldn't be like her. You care too much for the people around you. Your father had to be proud of you, he couldn't be anything else."

She craned her neck so she could look up into his face, a smile playing at the corner of her lips. "Thanks."

"It's true."

Taking a finger, he tipped her chin up so that she could see he was dead serious. Her eyes darkened, the deepest forest-green he'd ever seen. Her lips, lush, tempting, parted. A breath, somewhere between a sigh of contentment and a sound of surrender, leaked out.

"Did you go to see them while I was sleeping?"

Chase looked down at her and couldn't lie even as he knew it would make her angry. "Yes."

"Did you learn anything?"

"Mr. Nesmith wasn't the man behind the wheel."

Sabrina's eyes narrowed as she considered him for several moments. "I should be mad at you for going there alone."

"I wasn't in any danger. He was outside in the yard. I knew before I spoke to him that it wasn't him."

"So why did you stay and talk?"

"Because I had to."

Her head slowly slid up and down his thigh in a nod of understanding. Her lips turned up at the corners into the smallest, most angelically tempting smile.

He let out the breath he'd been holding. He'd expected her to be upset with him, at the very least troubled. Instead, she seemed to recognize why it had been important for him to stay and talk to the man.

What he didn't expect was her eyes to begin to smolder and spark as she suddenly said, "Make love to me."

"No."

"What do you mean, no?"

"You're sick. Somehow I don't think strenuous exercise would be what the doctor ordered right now." He grinned down at her, couldn't stop the mischievous slant to the turn of his own lips. Or the urge to tease her just a little.

One eyebrow shot up in challenge and warning before she rose to her knees, her palms centered squarely on his chest.

"Why don't you let *me* decide what I need?"

12

RINA STRADDLED his body.

Her blood sizzled through her veins, popping, burning and carrying a painful pleasure that settled into her core.

She'd fought him at every turn, giving in to the passion between them only reluctantly. She was tired of fighting.

Fighting herself and her fears. At the moment it was easier to take…to give in to the bubbling, roiling urges inside.

They were alone, here, tonight, and Chase had been so sweet. Comforting. Where her father had been stern and disapproving, he'd been gentle and kind.

She probably could have fought the crackle of sexual attraction that always raced across her skin in his presence. Rina couldn't fight his kindness and understanding.

And she wanted him. With a fierceness that bordered on torture. It was that simple.

"I don't think this is a good idea,"

They were both still fully clothed, but Rina could feel the hard ridge of his arousal snuggled tight against her body. There was something agonizing about knowing he was close, so close, but that she couldn't touch him. Not yet.

"I'm not paying you to think."

"You're not paying me at all."

"Semantics." She grinned down at him, rubbing her body against his, denim-on-denim friction.

His quick, indrawn breath echoed through her own body, a reverberating sound that twanged the sensitive nerves at the surface of her skin. It caressed her. As she knew his hands and mouth would if she persisted.

"Take off your shirt."

Chase studied her for several seconds, then said, "No." Grasping her hips, he lifted her off and away. Her feet hit the plush carpet.

"You need to rest, Sabrina."

Backing slowly away from him and the bed, Rina considered. His body was long, lean, honed by years of grueling training. She knew what he hid beneath the shirt and jeans he was using as armor against her. But they couldn't hide everything. In fact, the tight denim left not a thing to her imagination…and it was pretty damn good.

She tilted her head sideways. An idea sparked in her mind and a wicked smile pulsed at her lips.

"All right." Walking to the bedside table, she played with the clock radio the hotel had placed there. Music filled the room with the flick of her finger, some pop princess wailing against her ears.

Frowning, she played with the dials until she found exactly what she wanted, a pulse-pounding rock song. The smile slipped back into place as she realized what song was playing, Bon Jovi's "Lay Your Hands On Me." How perfect.

"If you won't take your clothes off…" She moved to stand at the foot of the bed. "Then I suppose I'll just have to take mine off instead."

The bass melded with her blood, her heart beating in time with the backbone of the song. Her body moved, instinctively finding the underlying rhythm. Her hips swayed as the words melted into the room.

Her eyes connected with his, dark and swirling, an unforgiving ocean enthralled by a storm. Her hands found the edge of her shirt and shifted it against her flat stomach. Cotton had never felt so good against her skin.

She bunched it together as her palms played. His gaze followed her every move, her hands on her ribs, abs, arms. The twist of her hips against tight jeans.

Her voice whispered the words, taunting, teasing, tempting, as she pulled her shirt over her head and threw it. Chase caught it midair, slapping it to the floor without ever taking his eyes from her.

Turning, she reached behind to unhook her bra, holding the cups with a single arm across her body. The straps slipped down her arms and the elastic hung loosely at her sides. She tossed a look at him over her shoulder before letting it slide all the way to the floor at her feet.

She could hear his deep intake of breath. And let a smile of triumph show through.

Instead of turning to treat him to her aching breasts, she kept her body facing away, rolling her neck and letting her hair sweep down the length of her back.

Warm sunlight leaked through the closed blinds, the day and the outside world shut firmly away. Maybe that's what gave her the courage to slowly unzip her jeans. She'd never have acted this way with any other man. Never had. Chase was the only one to call to the unrestrained side she tried so hard to deny. With him she couldn't help but let it go, be herself.

Rolling her hips in time, with the music and desire echoing through her, Rina let the denim skim away. Cold air touched her heated skin.

She had no idea when he moved. She hadn't heard the creak of the bed or the tread of his feet. One second his eyes had been devouring her—she could feel their touch—the next his hands were on her, hard and demanding.

"Witch." He breathed the single word into her ear right before his teeth raked down the curve of her neck to nip at her shoulder. A shudder coursed through her body. Passion pulsed from him, in time to the beat swirling around them, a beat of their own.

The song changed. She no longer cared.

Turning in his arms, she demanded again, "Take off your shirt."

She enjoyed the ripple of muscle in his chest and arms as he leaned back to jerk it over his head. His skin was tanned, a dark, luscious brown, the reflection of desert sand. She tried not to think about where that gorgeous color had come from. It didn't matter. It looked damn good on him.

He was healthy, virile, one-hundred-and-ten-percent male. And he called to a secret part of herself she acknowledged only with him.

His mouth found her again, crushing her in a way that should have left her unsettled but only made her think fuzzily, *mine*.

She filled her palms with him, letting her hands roam at will down his wide shoulders, over his toned biceps and across his tight abs. The valleys and planes of his chest intrigued her. Her fingernail flicked over the flat disc of his nipple. The muscles at his belly contracted and the tight center rose to meet her, eager for more of the punishment.

Leaning forward, she placed her mouth there. The scrape of her tongue against him sent a spike of need through her. Such a simple taste of him and her body was already tight with an unforgiving ache.

His hands drove into her hair, cupping her head and holding her close. She trailed her mouth up his body, scraping her teeth along the tendon in his neck on a journey back toward his lips.

Swinging her into his arms, he walked to the bed and placed her gently in the center.

His gaze was fierce and full of fire as he looked down at her, an inarticulate expression of his need for her. Quickly removing the rest of their clothes, he caressed her with nothing more than a sweeping look at her body. A tremor rambled down her spine, slow, unhurried and increasingly intense.

She arched toward him, tempting him to touch and taste before pulling out of his reach. As he watched her play with him his jaw tightened, a tic jumping just below his cheekbone. His erection swelled against the open cradle of her body and a gloriously revealing smile teased at her lips.

His hands and mouth were rough as he claimed her.

His lips sucked at her distended nipples, coaxing them tighter. Warmth melted through her, pooling at the center of her body.

"A man can only take so much," he mumbled against her skin.

She opened her mouth to say…something, but closed it when his lips touched down at the center of her belly. His tongue dipped into her navel and a jolt of electricity blasted straight to her sex.

His breath and mouth and tongue were so close to where she wanted—no, needed—them most. But he wouldn't go any farther. Instead, he tortured and teased her. Driving her insane. Playing at the curve of her hip, the dip of her belly, the crease of her thigh.

"There's only so much *this* woman can take." Her words were ragged and breathless.

His chuckle tickled her skin and her stomach tightened.

"Oh, I think you can handle more. You sure as hell know how to handle me."

He climbed back up her body, his mouth finding hers once more. She let out a whimper of protest, one that he swallowed as it turned into a gasp of need. His fingers found her, wet, hot and waiting.

He thrust a single finger inside her, all the breath leaking from her body as he let out a groan of his own.

His finger slid in and out as his thumb rubbed rhythmically against her clit. Tension built inside her, his hand swirling against her sex.

She was wild and wanton, uninhibited and sexy. But only with Chase. With Chase she was free.

The pleasure he gave her was almost unbearable. If he didn't stop soon she was going to explode in his hand. But that wasn't what she wanted.

She wanted him, flush with her body, a part of her.

Her muscles tingled and pulsed. She recognized the signs of an impending orgasm. "Stop. No. I want you inside me."

The words were difficult to say, but somehow she found the strength to utter them as she fought the slippery edge of release.

Rina watched as he ripped his jeans away. He reached into a bag that he'd set on the dresser and pulled out a foil packet. Rolling a condom down over himself, he quickly rejoined her on the bed.

In a single, smooth thrust he slid high and tight inside her body, the sensation exquisite. With deliberate strokes, he sent her hurtling toward the edge of reason only to violently jerk her back. Steady pressure paired with unexpected moments of stillness that drove her utterly mad.

She had no idea how long he kept her poised on the brink of orgasm, teetering back and forth between reality and abandon. Her head thrashed against the pillows, her body weeping at their connection.

Finally, unable to take it anymore, she wrapped her legs around his body, driving her heels into his thighs and holding him to her. Rina pushed her body as hard and high as it would go, taking as much of him as she could get.

"Chase." The single word sounded like a prayer. One he answered when he thrust deep, finally breaking the unbearable tension. Sensation swirled inside her in ever-tightening circles. Her body convulsed beneath him for what felt like forever, pulsing and pulling, a keening cry breaking free from her throat.

Somewhere in the back of her mind she registered his own release and the whisper of his voice in her ear, "Sabrina," sounding strangely like a prayer of his own.

Never in her life had that single word sounded so good.

CHASE WATCHED her sleep. She was so peaceful. The never-ending drive that always seemed to keep her on edge had eased. She was beautiful, formidable, on a regular day. But seeing her here, now, snuggled next to his body...trusting.

That was the difference. She'd let her guard down. Just long enough for it to devastate him.

He'd never met a woman he could imagine as part of his life. And now he could never imagine his life without Sabrina.

He was in love with his wife. Who would have ever thought that could be a problem?

Most people hoped for this moment in their lives. Yet here he was, tied to the most amazing, beautiful, honest woman he'd ever met, and she didn't want to be married to him.

She was scared. He realized that. But what scared the hell out of *him* was that he didn't know how to take her fear away. And if he couldn't do that then he'd lose her. As simple as that.

She wanted him. She even liked him. Did she love him? He wasn't sure.

What he needed was time to convince her. Time for the fear to ease, for her to realize he wasn't going anywhere and their lives could be happy and satisfying.

She'd finally opened her body to him, not because she couldn't control the sexual sparks between them but because she'd wanted him. At least it was a step in the right direction. She'd seduced him, quite well actually, instead of him chasing her like a mindless teenager in heat.

Sabrina stirred beside him, mumbling something unintelligible before settling back down again, her arm thrown possessively across his chest. The muscles beneath tightened, squeezing painfully.

He was scared out of his mind. He'd been in war, flown aerial combat maneuvers with the best pilots, had ejected from a malfunctioning plane, and watched as people around him died. He'd survived it all, even thrived on the danger sometimes.

But the thought of losing the woman beside him terrified him.

He was about to enter the fiercest battle of his life, the fight for his wife. And one wrong move could cost him everything.

RINA WALKED up to the front door of her apartment, the medicine she'd taken a few hours before dulling her gait just a little. It tended to make her drowsy, which, on a flight, was usually a good thing. Today, she wasn't entirely sure. Her world had already seemed a bit fuzzy, out of focus. Loose.

Chase shadowed her, his steps echoing comfortably with her own in the quiet afternoon. The sun was just starting to set, glaring directly into her eyes and making her squint. And he was there, at her back. Always.

Waking up beside Chase this morning had been a double-edged sword. On one hand, the feel of his body next to hers, warm and solid had been more than tempting. Not just physically, but emotionally. She could seriously get used to having him around. But she couldn't do that. Could not allow herself to fall in love with her husband.

It would hurt too much.

Something told her it would be so easy to do, to give her heart to this man. But they both had too much to lose, careers, reputations…pieces of herself.

The more she said it, the more the excuses sounded flimsy even to her own ears. Yes, the potential to lose everything they'd both worked for was there—that was reality. What she was having trouble believing was that the sacrifice wouldn't be worth it.

The more she thought about it, the more she wondered if, in order to be able to call Chase her own, she'd give up a hell of a lot more than a career she wasn't even certain she wanted anymore.

But she didn't have to make that choice right now, today. No. There were things she needed to think about, think about with a clear head. She couldn't do that now.

What she could do was take advantage of the fact that neither of them had to work, and her husband was standing at her front door, watching her with tempting eyes.

She could invite him in to her apartment, have her wicked way with him. It had been a line she hadn't wanted to let him cross. But now, that didn't seem so important. The only thing that she could think about was how to haul him inside if he wouldn't come willingly.

"Do you want to come in?"

He stared at her for several moments. Rina's heart was beating against her ribs by the time he finally said, "Yes."

She turned the knob at her back, unwilling to take her eyes away from him for even a second. The door burst in behind her and she nearly tripped over the raised edge. Chase reached out for her, grabbing her elbow and steadying her. They backed slowly inside. He closed the door deliberately behind them. But instead of jumping her like she wanted, he looked away from her, taking in her space.

She saw it through his eyes—frilly maybe? Girlie, definitely. She'd spent so many years trying to build a home for her father. He hadn't appreciated her efforts. But she did. This was the one place she felt…comfortable. Relieved.

Navy and clear crystal beads hung from a pair of matched lamps, catching the waning sunlight through her lace-edged curtains and throwing rainbows onto the jeweled boxes lined up on a corner bookshelf. A set of rose-patterned china was perfectly arranged on an antique rolling cart in the corner. It was something she'd indulged in several years ago. Something she'd never had but always longed for as a child.

She'd desperately wanted to be able to play dress-up with her mother's clothes and jewelry, to host a tea party like the other little girls who'd streamed in and out of her life. But her father hadn't let her have a tea set. He'd always said it would just get broken during a move. She would have much preferred having it and losing it than never having it at all.

So when she'd seen the set in an antique-store window, she'd bought it.

But now, watching Chase stare at it, his mouth slightly open, she thought maybe the impulse had been a mistake. Bright pink color whooshed up her skin. She could feel the heat of embarrassment and wished she had the power to pull it back. But she didn't.

"Oh, shut your mouth before you catch flies."

He turned to look at her, a calculating gleam in his eyes that made her heart stutter in her chest for just a second.

"You hide this side of yourself well, Captain…Carden."
He reached for her, pulling her soundly into his arms and
trapping her exactly as he wanted…as she wanted, too.

Rina fought conflicting emotions: an unsettling feeling of
exposure—something told her he saw much more than she'd
ever intended to reveal—and the undeniable urge to rip the
man's shirt off so she could feel his body against her own.

Ripping sounded more fun so she went with that.

Threading her fingers through the buttons at the front of
his shirt, she let her fingertips play. She enjoyed the contrast
of his smooth, heated skin and the roughness of his hair. His
own hands worked inside the pockets of her jeans, cupping
her ass and pulling her tighter into his body.

He was aroused. But then so was she. Nothing more
than the simple anticipation of what was to come and she
was already hot and slick with wanting him. She could feel
the slippery sensation between her thighs as she shifted in
his embrace.

Unbuttoning his shirt, she let it slip from his shoulders and
fall to the floor at his back. She didn't wait for him to recip-
rocate but reached between their bodies and pulled the hem
of her own shirt up and over her head. Her bra followed,
dropping between them with a muffled plop.

His hands were everywhere, plucking and pulling, soothing
and caressing. Sensations shot through her, overloading her
nervous system and sending her into pleasure meltdown.

Unsnapping her jeans, he pushed them down her legs and
knelt between her open thighs. He snagged the edge of her
panties to pull them down as well. Resting her hands on his
shoulders, she let him take her weight as he discarded both.

She watched as he rose, his eyes traveling the entire length
of her body, worshipping. She'd never had anyone, any man,
look at her with that unnerving mixture. Part need to devour,

part drive to possess, part absolute adoration. It was intoxicating, and possibly addictive.

She could easily crave this every damn day.

Taking his hand, Rina tugged and took a step toward her bedroom. He resisted, shook his head and said, "No."

Instead, he coaxed her over to the couch and pressed her onto the fluffy cushions. It looked delicate, old, with its carved claw-foot legs and curved back. But its look was deceiving—it was actually very comfortable. The faux velvet wrapped around her body, softly caressing her skin. She would have much preferred the feel of Chase as he slid inside her.

She reached for him, pulling at the waistband of his jeans, hoping to catch him off balance and topple him down with her. But he didn't. The man was sturdier than he looked—and he looked pretty damn sturdy. Instead he reached over her. She heard a rustle but couldn't twist her head far enough to see.

"Somehow, I never pictured you as a crystal type of girl."

Chase brought a line of the beads she'd strung onto wire before hanging around the bottom edge of her lamp. It had been a fanciful touch that had made her happy.

"I should have, though. You like to hide it, don't you? Behind the precise lines of your uniform and the regs that you let govern your life. But I should have seen beneath all that." Chase moved the crystals back and forth above her body. Sunlight flashed into her eyes. "So pretty."

His fingers touched her skin, softly gliding across the rainbow he'd reflected there. He traced the glowing patch of color as he shifted it across her body.

She gasped as he grazed a distended nipple and she arched her back for more. Instead, he moved the crystals closer, letting the tiny knot at the end touch the very tip of one breast. The cold contact and the scraping sensation as he trailed it in a widening circle across her body sent her up in flames.

He'd barely touched her and yet, she knew if he pushed inside her at this precise moment she'd fly apart in his arms.

Grabbing the crystals, she startled him enough that he let go when her hands wrapped around the cool glass. Flinging them to the floor, she reached again for the waistband of his jeans. This time she wouldn't let him elude her. Quickly working down the fly, she pushed her hand into the opening, relishing the way his erection jumped as she got closer.

Looking up at him with a mischievous grin, she wished she hadn't been so hasty in throwing the string of crystals away. She could reach behind her and grab another but…she had a better plan in mind.

Pushing the denim and boxer briefs to the floor, she sat up, pulling her feet beneath her, and urged him onto the cushions beside her. He settled back easily, watching her, waiting to see what she'd do.

She didn't disappoint either of them when she dropped smoothly onto him, impaling herself on his erection, inch by preciously slow inch.

He groaned as she melted over him, thrusting hard and deep inside her when she didn't move quickly enough for him. She relished every movement as strong and urgent fingers gripped her hips and rocked them both together.

Unable to do anything but hang on and enjoy the ride, Rina wrapped her arms tight around his neck as he buried his face in the valley of her breasts. His mouth latched onto one nipple, not in a smooth and soft caress but with the biting edge of teeth.

The room began to fade to black around her, bursts of light shooting through her peripheral vision before creeping in to take over everything. Her eyes closed and her body shuddered on the first tremors of an orgasm. She spasmed again and again before Chase finally joined her, throwing back his head and thrusting so high her knees left the cushions.

In the back of her mind she thought, *This is the only time I'll enjoy flying,* before collapsing onto his chest. She was utterly boneless, unable to move or think.

Pulling her tight against his body, Chase's damp chest rose and fell beneath her in a rhythm that matched her own labored breaths.

Finally, after who knows how long, he lifted his head and looked into her sleepy eyes. "Thank you."

"For what?"

"For letting me in."

Aw, hell was the only response she could think of.

13

DONALD STARED down at the unsmiling face on the newspaper print. It was similar to the photo Amy had taken upon completing basic training, but this one was clearly Carden's Thunderbird publicity photograph.

The flight suit and cap made him want to scream. He'd spent years of his life serving next to pilots, protecting them, and working in the security forces. And now this one, this same breed of man—who seemed to think he was better than everyone else simply because he could invert a plane in the clouds—had taken his baby girl.

Donald's eyes skimmed the words on the page again. He'd read the article in depth repeatedly; now his gaze simply jumped from one fragmented word to another.

Hero…savior…President…ceremony.

His eyes landed on a quote from a Captain Rina McAllister, the public affairs officer for the squadron. "Major Carden is a hero to this nation and the United States Air Force is proud to honor him with the Distinguished Flying Cross."

He had to stop the ceremony. One way or another. Perhaps she could help. It was her job to protect the image of the air force, the image of the squadron. Surely, if she knew the truth, she'd put a stop to this farce.

But he'd also set plan B in motion. Next to the rest of the crooked and crinkled newspaper lay a card, snow-white like the ones he'd sent Carden. Only this one had the air force coat of arms, the Thunderbirds logo and a personalized invitation to the medal ceremony he was trying to stop.

Reaching beneath his seat, he checked to make sure both of his Berettas were safe and secure. He'd gotten on base several times now and no one had stopped to inspect his car. He'd drive onto base, to the location printed in black curling letters, and hide one of his guns.

Just in case. An airman was always prepared. Even a retired one.

HOME. It wasn't the same anymore, damn it. Rina had spent the morning getting ready for work, trying not to remember what she and Chase had done on her sofa. And in her bed. And on her kitchen counter. And in the shower this morning before he'd left for his own apartment to grab a clean uniform.

She'd been fighting the urge to look for him all morning. It scared her.

She couldn't concentrate. And this couldn't have happened at a worse possible time. His ceremony was this Friday. It needed all her attention and focus. Instead, her mind kept drifting back to the weekend they'd just shared, how he'd comforted her, cherished her, made her feel beautiful and sexy—something she'd never imagined about herself…except with Chase.

If anything, the realization that he was taking over only cemented her resolve more. She couldn't let that happen. They had no future. Their relationship couldn't last for so many reasons.

They'd put the cart before the horse and now there was no going back. Marriages needed a hell of a lot more than sex to make them work.

Look at her parents. They'd loved each other at one point—or so her father had said—and everything had still turned to shit.

Sure, she and Chase might have been able to have a few weeks or months. If it weren't for the effect it could have on their careers.

They had a spark, a connection but it would fizzle out. Just like her parents had. The blaze of sexual attraction felt amazing but she didn't want to stick around for the crash and burn.

So why did she care that he hadn't come into her office this morning?

She didn't.

Gritting her teeth, Rina vowed to make the statement true.

And she sure as hell wouldn't seek him out. No, that was an urge she couldn't give in to.

The phone rang. Rina jumped with guilt. She'd been staring blankly at her computer screen for at least fifteen minutes. The air force didn't pay her to dissect her relationship…or lack of one. Shaking her head, she picked up the phone.

"Captain, you must stop the medal ceremony."

Sabrina's eyebrows wrinkled. "I'm sorry, sir. I don't understand. Who are you?"

"That doesn't matter. Major Carden doesn't deserve that medal. You must stop the ceremony. If you knew what he'd done…"

Realization smacked Rina flat across the face. This was the man, the man who'd hit Chase with his car.

She wanted so badly to scream in his ear, to tell him what an excuse for skin he was. But she couldn't do that. Not if she hoped to keep the man on the line long enough to learn something useful.

"Sir, I'm sure you understand—the ceremony is in four

days. Arrangements are well underway. I can't simply cancel a ceremony, specifically one the President is planning to attend, without something more concrete."

Silence met her words. She waited, her heartbeat speeding to something resembling Mach one—or what she imagined breaking the sound barrier felt like.

"He killed my baby girl." The words were soft, before they came again, more forceful and louder. "He killed my baby girl."

"That's a very serious allegation." Rina's mind was racing. How to get him to give her his name…at least if they had that they could get the authorities involved and *do* something. As it was, she was calling the commander the minute this conversation was over whether Chase liked it or not. The man was obviously delusional. She ached for his loss…but he clearly needed help. Before he did something drastic like really try to kill Chase.

"Can you be more specific?"

"Just…just look into the events of that night. He wasn't a hero. He left people alone, in the dark, to die."

The line went dead. Rina cursed. Slamming it down into the cradle, she immediately snatched it back up and made two phone calls—the first to Chase, the second to their commander.

Chase arrived first.

"What the hell do you think you're doing?"

"What you should have done weeks ago."

Following just minutes behind was Commander Wright.

Rina motioned him into the chair behind her desk, knowing that giving him the power position could only gain her points— precious points she and Chase might need. She was about to make the man pretty angry. He wasn't known for his easygoing personality. He was somewhat of a stickler for the chain of command…something he had in common with her father.

Chase had stomped all over it by not reporting the threats when they'd first arrived. And she'd helped him so they were both about to get tarred with the same brush.

It wasn't going to be pleasant.

Walking across the room, she closed her door as Chase stared daggers at her.

"Want to tell me what's going on? What do you mean a security breach? The President of the United States is going to be here in less than four days."

"Sir, in recent weeks, Chase has received several threatening letters."

Wright's gaze swiveled to take in Chase, now standing at stark attention, staring straight ahead.

"Is this correct?"

"Yes, sir."

"And you're just now telling me about this? Both of you?" His voice rose to a pitch loud enough to rattle the windows in their frames.

She could have mentioned that she'd only found out about them herself but it didn't matter. She'd decided not to contact Wright immediately so she was as much to blame as Chase.

"I didn't want to cause the person any more pain, sir. They lost a loved one the night of my crash."

"That's bullshit, Major, and you know it. You put lives at risk by not reporting this. I want details and I want them right now. After that we'll discuss the ramifications of this little stunt."

HE WAS ANGRY with her. She knew that. But, given the chance, Rina would have done the exact same thing over again.

They had increased the security detail surrounding the squadron and specifically for that night. The Secret Service had been informed—they hadn't been any happier about being kept in the dark than the commander had been. And people with more investigative experience than they had were now trying to track down the name Chase had reluctantly given them.

For the first time since she'd watched that car barrel into Chase, Rina began to breathe easier; not perfectly, but a little lighter at least.

She'd followed him to his place. It was the second time in their weird and tumultuous relationship that she was the pursuer instead of the pursued.

How many times had he sought her out when she hadn't wanted to see him?

Well, tough cookies if he didn't want to talk to her right now. It was his turn.

At his front door, he turned and stared at her with cold, blank eyes.

"Go home, Sabrina."

The words hurt less than the expression on his face.

"No."

Unwilling to leave things the way they were, she grabbed the front of his shirt, shoved him back against the door and fused her mouth to his.

She could taste his anger and a self-torment beneath that made her heart ache. She didn't understand exactly what he was going through, but she understood the guilt, felt it each and every time she thought of her mother.

Her mere existence had contributed to her mother's unhappiness. She could no longer focus on her own whims…she'd had to focus on a child's. A job that in the end she'd decided she didn't want. The fact that her birth had made her mother's life difficult hadn't been Rina's fault but that didn't stop the emotions, the guilt. Just like the death of those six soldiers wasn't Chase's fault, but it didn't stop him from dwelling on them anyway, of feeling that he owed them, their families, something he really didn't.

Her heart fluttered painfully in her chest, like a bird tearing at a wire wrapped around its foot, until Chase's hands finally reached for her. They weren't soft and coaxing, but grasped her around the waist and dug in as if he never wanted to let her go. Then and only then did her pulse settle back to something normal—at least normal for being wrapped in Chase.

Her lips were battered and swollen but she didn't care. Tears, she had no idea where they'd come from, welled in the corners of her eyes.

Jerking back, she took a long, deep breath.

"I'm sorry, Chase. But I couldn't take the chance of anything else happening to you."

"I was just hoping it wouldn't come to this. I knew if anyone else got involved I wouldn't have control over it anymore. I can't help feeling that somehow I've taken something tragic and turned it into a catastrophe."

"No, Chase. He turned it into a catastrophe. He needs help. And that's what he's going to get when we find him." Hopefully before the man hurt Chase again.

His phone rang. Glancing down at the cell hooked to his waist, he said, "It's the commander," as he pulled it out to answer. He listened slowly, his eyes narrowing, before saying, "Thanks for letting me know."

He hung up and looked at Rina. "They've found the motel where Blankenship is staying—the Desert Sand. But he isn't there and the guy at the front desk hasn't seen him all day. The room appears almost empty—no suitcase or bag. They're worried he's left."

"Damn it!"

She swirled away from him, anger and frustration coursing through her body. When was this going to end?

His arms wrapped around her. Gently, he pulled her back, tucking her head beneath his chin.

"So, does this mean you were worried about me?"

"Of course."

"Does this mean you'd be upset if I disappeared from your life?"

She let the answer slip quietly from her lips into his shoulder. "Yes."

"Does this mean you'll let me be your husband for real? That you'll tear up those papers and forget about an annulment?"

"Maybe." She was willing to think about it. "But not until after the ceremony. Let's get this whole thing behind us. Besides, I think if the commander found out right now that we'd been keeping this a secret, too, there'd be no help for it. We'd be booted on our asses so fast our heads would spin."

"Fair enough."

Reaching behind him, Chase pulled open the door to his apartment.

"Can we at least practice our conjugal rights until then?"

A smile tugged at the corners of her lips as desire melted slowly through her body.

"Absolutely."

THEY'D FOUND HIM. That wasn't good. At least he'd been taking his most important things in the car each time he left—if for no other reason than he was afraid someone might break in and steal everything he owned. The Desert Sand wasn't exactly in the best part of town.

Donald stayed low in the front seat of his car—a rental he'd picked up so Carden wouldn't recognize it. The windows were open and, from his vantage point in front of the man's neighbors, he'd been able to hear every word they spoke on the front porch.

What worried him was that they knew his name. They'd obviously finally called in the big guns. He'd have to be extra careful now.

But something else had stuck out from the conversation he'd just overheard, something that surprised him.

Carden was married. Nothing he'd read about the man had ever mentioned a wife. In fact, he knew for certain that Oprah had asked about his personal life six weeks before and he hadn't mentioned it.

The woman was obviously air force; she was in uniform. He wondered who she was.

It wouldn't take much to find out. A quick trip to the marriage bureau. He'd go first thing in the morning. Having information was never a bad thing.

If nothing else, it sounded like Carden wanted to keep his marriage a secret for the moment.

They'd see about that.

14

"BITCH!"

The single word roared into Rina's ear, drowning out everything else and leaving her speechless.

She gripped the phone in her hand and dropped like a rock into the chair behind her desk. She'd been busy handling details for the ceremony, about to go and look at the auditorium and check to make sure the advance team from the Secret Service didn't need anything.

She hadn't been prepared for this. In fact, after spending last night with Chase, she'd been pretty happy.

"I gave that information to you because I thought you'd do the right thing. I should have known better. You're married to him. You'd never do the right thing. You're covering it all up. You're just as guilty as he is.

"What would everyone say, what would General McAllister say if he knew about your marriage? You're going to be sorry. Both of you. I'll make sure of that."

Rina opened her mouth over and over like a fish out of water. Nothing came out but a squeak. And then the line was dead and she had no one to say the words to anyway.

Oh, shit came to mind.

It had obviously been Blankenship. He'd been angry. Screaming at her. Mindless with rage. Her heart pounded fast in her chest, the same feeling of fear she'd gotten when she'd heard about Chase's crash, when she'd seen that car clip him.

"Son of a bitch." The man knew that they were married.

"What's wrong?"

She hadn't heard Chase come in. She hadn't seen him in...four hours? Somehow it was fitting that he'd chosen this precise moment to walk into her office. The precise moment she wanted him most, the moment she should be pushing him away.

Standing up from her chair, she walked over to her door and shut it tight. Taking him by the arm, Rina pulled him over and pressed him back against the wood.

A familiar fire lit in the back of his ocean blue eyes, a sparkle that started an instant chain reaction inside her body. Sex wasn't what she needed right now, although it probably would have bled off some of the adrenaline pumping into her blood.

Instead, she wrapped shaky arms around his waist, laid her head on his chest and buried her face into his body. He immediately grabbed for her, cocooning her in his warmth, his protection, his scent.

"You're scaring me. What happened?"

Rina just shook her head. In a minute she would tell him. Right now, she needed some of his strength. Just a tiny infusion for her own.

"Your father. Is he okay?"

"Yes." The word was muffled against the starched cotton of his shirt.

"Sadie?"

"Fine."

Apparently satisfied that no one was in immediate danger, Chase tightened his hold on her and simply waited. After a few minutes, she slowly let go, disengaging herself from his body inch by reluctant inch. When she was finally one giant step away, she looked up at him.

He stared back, silent and intense. He looked ready to chew nails or kick some serious ass, whichever would fix what was wrong. In that moment, he reminded her more of her father than she'd thought possible.

"Now will you tell me what's wrong?"

"Blankenship called back. He's mad. At me. And he knows we're married."

Chase wanted to smash something. Preferably the asshole who'd just called Sabrina and scared the hell out of her.

He'd never seen her like that. Vulnerable, yes. Sick and miserable, yes. Shaken to the core? No. She was one of the strongest people he'd ever met. Nothing fazed her. Whatever Blankenship had said to her…it hadn't been good.

He'd been willing to take some shit off the man; he deserved it. He'd been willing to take some measure of risk with his own safety and well-being. But he sure as hell wasn't willing to stand by and let the man threaten and scare his wife.

That was where Chase drew the line.

"Tell me everything. Word for word."

She walked across her office once before backtracking to sit down in her chair. She tugged at the hem of her skirt, straightened the lapels on her shirt. He could practically see the internal armor she was putting back in place.

"He opened with *bitch.*"

"Son of a—"

"No. Just plain *bitch.* He screamed it in my ear. Then he basically told me I'd betrayed him because I hadn't done anything with the information he'd given me yesterday and that my father would not like that I was protecting my husband instead of doing the honorable thing. And then he threatened us both."

His jaw tightened and his teeth grated together. "Anything else?"

"Don't you think that's enough?" She turned angry eyes toward him.

Good. That, Chase could take. It was the fear he'd seen when he'd walked in the door that scared him spitless.

"He knows we're married. And he apparently knows who my father is. Soon the General will know we're married, along with everyone else. Not to mention that this nutcase is trying to ruin your award ceremony and my career in one fell swoop. And intends bodily injury or death to you, me or both of us."

Chase really didn't care about the ceremony. But he did care about Sabrina.

"Cancel the ceremony."

"No."

"I don't want the medal. I don't deserve it."

"The hell you don't. But even if I did, it wouldn't stop him. Not now."

Her words made him feel…powerless. He didn't like that at all. There must be a way to stop the maniac.

"You don't know that."

"Yes, I do. You didn't hear him. Whatever is going on in his mind, this man is angry and unhinged. Not a great combination."

Sabrina ran her fingers over her hair, patting imaginary strands into place. He watched her eyebrows knit and a groove of worry dig into her skin. At least there was one thing he could do.

"I'm taking you out of this equation."

Sabrina looked at him, hard. "No. You're not."

"I won't put you in danger."

"You have no authority over me and my job decisions, Major."

Crap. Chase squinted his eyes and rubbed at the headache forming behind his temples. If he pushed her on this…he'd lose every last speck of ground he'd gained with her over the last few weeks. She was finally starting to see him—to see them—as something real and concrete.

If he insisted, she'd never forgive him for taking away her damned sense of control—over herself, her life, her career choices. He wondered when she'd figure out life couldn't always be controlled.

The Secret Service was here. Everyone was aware of the situation. He'd stay glued to her side for the next two days.

"Fine. On one condition. You stay with me. And at the first sign of trouble you get the hell out of the way."

She glared at him.

"Promise me or I'm calling the President's office myself."

"Fine." She sighed, a resigned sound that had never sounded so good in his life. "What about our marriage?"

"What about it?"

"He knows about it, Chase. And he has no problem using that information against us. Somehow, he's figured out that no one knows—including the air force. It's not going to stay a secret for very long."

Her eyes narrowed as she paused for a moment.

"We need to file the paperwork now. At least that way, when all hell breaks loose, we can look like we were taking steps to correct the problem—correct the prank gone wrong that it was," she said.

"Our marriage is not a prank." At least not to him. But if she could still call it that after everything they'd shared, been through together lately…

"No, it isn't, Chase, but it also isn't the best thing for either of us right now."

"I'm not signing anything, Sabrina. There's got to be another way." A way that didn't involve losing the woman he loved.

He couldn't read the thoughts or emotions swirling behind her eyes. God, he wanted to, but once again she was shutting him out.

"Promise me you won't do anything rash."

Nothing. A blank wall of nothing. Her mouth didn't even twitch with a desire to give him that assurance.

"Sabrina Carden, if you care at all for me, for our relationship, don't do this. Don't do something we'll both regret."

SHE CARED. She cared too much. She cared enough to do the right thing, no matter how much it hurt.

Rina submitted the divorce paperwork—without Chase's signature or his knowledge. He was being stubborn and, whether he realized it now or not, he'd thank her later, whenever the shit hit the fan and they had proof that the problem would soon be a nonissue.

So why did she feel like crap? Like she'd somehow betrayed him...or herself?

It was the best thing for them both. It was certainly the best move for their careers. And if she was starting to question whether the life she'd mapped out with the air force was really what she wanted...she knew Chase wouldn't ever change his mind. He was career air force, flyboy all the way. And he'd resent her and their relationship if it cost him the one thing that mattered.

Just like her mother had resented the loss of her freedom. And her father had resented being thrust into the role of single father. She wouldn't live a life of regret and resentment. Not now. Not with Chase.

The ceremony was tomorrow and if she could just make it through the next few days...things would calm down. Things would get better. Maybe—maybe—they could start over from scratch. Try dating and fooling around a little without the pressure of knowing their joke had consequences that neither of them had planned.

"Captain McAllister."

Rina's head shot up from staring unseeingly at her desk, startled by the voice of her father coming through the open doorway to her office.

"Sir? What…what are you doing here?"

He strolled inside, ramrod straight and in perfect order. Ever the General.

"You don't think I'd miss Major Carden's award ceremony, do you?"

Of course he'd been invited; she'd sent the invitation herself. But for some reason she'd never thought he'd actually attend. And he certainly hadn't given her a heads-up that he was coming into town. Apparently, his secretary had forgotten to call her.

"Besides, I couldn't pass up the opportunity to see my little girl."

He didn't move toward her. He didn't smile. Just once, despite the fact that they were both in uniform and it was against the rules, she'd like her father to show her some affection. To hug her, kiss her on the cheek, anything. To put her above the air force and protocol.

But he wouldn't. She knew that. It didn't seem to stop her from wanting. Just like knowing she couldn't stay married to Chase didn't stop her from hoping in the deepest corners of her soul.

"I'm not little anymore." Somehow he seemed to miss that she'd grown up while he was away, preoccupied, busy with his career goals.

"I know you're busy handling details. I won't interfere."

Of course he wouldn't. Nothing could interfere with air force business, not even him.

"Maybe we can get together later this evening. Here's the hotel where I'm staying."

She had a perfectly good spare bedroom. She'd originally gotten the two-bedroom with her father in mind. She should have known he wouldn't have imposed…even on her.

"Certainly, sir. I'll cook dinner. Seven o'clock?".

With a nod he walked back out her door. The first time she'd seen him in almost a year, and not a hug, not a how-are-you, he hadn't even called her by her name.

This couldn't get any worse. She'd waited for days for the other shoe to drop but she knew…it was dropping tomorrow night, in the middle of the biggest project of her entire air force career, in front of her commander, several generals, the President of the United States and her father.

The shit was going to hit the fan. Everything was going to go up in smoke.

And the only thing that she really cared about was that when the haze finally cleared she'd no longer have Chase. He'd never forgive her for what she'd just done.

DONALD STARED at his old uniform, laid out on the dingy motel bed. It was pristine; years of habit were hard to break.

He'd wear it tonight, for his Amy. She'd always loved to see him pressed and dressed. As a little girl she'd danced around the room in his uniform jacket, a bright, perfect smile on her face.

Taking out the 9 mm Beretta, a virtual twin to the one he'd hidden just days ago on site, he ran his finger slowly down the length of the cold metal. He laid it beside his jacket, shirt and pants. It was simply part of the uniform for him, as a past security specialist. He'd spent years of his life teaching the new, up-and-coming airmen how to protect themselves in danger, how to hold steady and shoot straight.

Sitting in the rickety chair next to the particleboard table, Donald laid out his kit and began to disassemble the weapon. He rubbed each piece of the firearm as he oiled and cleaned it with loving care. He wouldn't be able to take this one inside with him tonight, but it deserved the same respect and attention anyway.

Placing it back together, he thought, tomorrow it would be all over. Tomorrow he'd finally be able to put his baby girl to rest. Everyone would understand and appreciate the sacrifice that she had made…they'd honor *her.*

He'd make sure of it.

THE DAY OF THE ceremony dawned clear and slightly chilly. Rina would know. She'd been unable to sleep and had watched the sun rise slowly over the horizon.

There was so much riding on this day. It was Chase's moment of glory and she wanted to make it perfect for him. Only the nasty churning in her stomach told her that probably wouldn't happen.

Had she made the right decision?

She wasn't sure. In a few short hours they'd know, though. Rising up out of bed, she started her routine wishing more than anything that Chase was beside her. Pushing the unwelcome thought away, she got ready for work and headed for the base.

She stopped to speak to the guard on duty to ensure that they'd all been given the updated alert for Donald Blankenship. They had.

She should feel safer. She didn't.

Rina spent the next several hours double-checking arrangements that had been made for weeks. Everything was in order. And still her skin crawled with nervous energy. She stood in the back of the auditorium and fidgeted with a clipboard in her hand. Her gaze raked across the empty space, looking for something, anything she might do.

"I know a way to bleed that off."

His voice melted over her as his arms circled her waist. She should have pulled away from him. Florists, caterers, Secret Service and airmen had been streaming in and out all day. They were in uniform and anyone could see them.

But she couldn't. The feel of his solid body at her back helped calm her nerves like nothing else had.

"Bleed off what?"

"The adrenaline. There's a reason people turn to each other for sex after a trauma."

"Is that what you did in Iraq?"

She had no idea where the question had come from. She had no right to ask. But it mattered. More than she wanted it to.

"No. You weren't there."

"You didn't know we were married."

"It doesn't matter, Sabrina." His warm breath touched the skin of her neck. His mouth found the hollow of her ear and dipped inside. "One night with you and I was ruined for anyone else. No one but you would do."

Her breath caught in her lungs. Did he really mean that or was he just trying to seduce her like always? With Chase she wasn't sure. She'd always been good at reading people, but with him, her emotions seemed to cloud her judgment.

"Of course, there weren't a lot of women to choose from."

"It wouldn't have mattered if a busload of naked women had jumped out and thrown themselves at my feet." He shifted behind her, turning her to face him. "From the moment I laid eyes on you again, I knew."

Chase cupped the back of her neck with both hands, his thumbs running along her cheekbones, soothing her nerves in a way she hadn't realized was possible. His mouth connected with hers in a soft kiss full of tenderness and banked fire.

"God, you have a way of just…running over my better judgment. I'm not myself around you."

"I think you're wrong. I think you're finally yourself around me."

It was true. She'd spent years forcing herself into a life plan that made her feel like a katydid with skin one size too small. She couldn't spread her wings, she couldn't fly.

With Chase, she wasn't afraid, not for herself. For him, yes, but she was sure that sensation would never go away, even if he was no longer a part of her life.

He stared down into her eyes. It was a study that she felt to the depths of her soul.

"I want you in my life, Sabrina. I want you as my wife. I've never been so sure of anything. Tonight, after all this is over, I want to talk about a life together. Will you think about it?"

She found herself nodding even though she knew it wouldn't happen.

The thought of staying married to this man…it tied her stomach in knots even the best navy man would be proud of. Part of her wanted nothing more than to spend the rest of her life bickering and making up with him. Part of her hoped that it could be true.

The rest of her realized that things were in motion, things she couldn't stop, things she *wouldn't* stop—for his sake— and they were likely going to destroy everything.

"We can talk about this tomorrow. Today is for you."

DONALD DROVE through the gates of the base, producing an ID he'd made just yesterday—Max Nesmith Senior. He knew the man had been invited. He knew all of the grieving families had been. It was a PR stunt with no real intention behind it. They'd expect anyone attending to sit quietly in the audience and just appreciate being given an invitation, to relish the idea of sitting in the same room with the President.

He could have cared less about that.

The security personnel confirmed his invitation and waved him onto the base with directions for where the auditorium was located. Not that he needed them.

He reached the parking lot, got out of his car and headed towards the lit entrance. People milled about outside, dressed in their peacock best. The mustache he'd bought at a local costume store itched. He ignored it.

Straightening his spine, he continued walking straight for the security personnel and the hulking white metal detectors that loomed over the open doorways. As he approached the guards standing on either side, he pulled out his retired military ID badge. It had taken him hours to alter his and yet more time to find a place that could produce a name tag similar to the air force regulations. But people were streaming around him and with the uniform no one looked very hard. People saw what they expected to see.

After a few sweaty moments while the airman studied his ID, he was waved into the entranceway.

Donald let out a sigh of relief. One hurdle down. Now all he needed to do was retrieve his gun.

CHASE SAT on the dais, staring out at a sea of people. Most of them he didn't know. Most of them didn't know him. But they'd come to watch the hero receive his medal.

The President sat on the dais several seats down, the senator to his right, the First Lady to his left. Secret Service surrounded everyone. He felt almost as if he was sitting on the outside of a bubble, which was just fine with him. The

President had stopped briefly to extend his congratulations and thanks. Chase had smiled, shaken his hand and immediately looked for Sabrina in the milling crowd.

It meant a lot to him that his sister and mother were here, in the first row, sharing this with him. He'd spent the afternoon with them because they were flying back out again first thing in the morning. He'd made sure that Sabrina was protected before he'd left, though. She might not have realized it, but several sets of eyes were watching her.

Now she sat several seats down from his family. She wore her mess dress uniform just as he did, equally spit polished and shined. She looked amazing. He sensed her nerves, quite possibly worse than his own, which was crazy considering in about five minutes he'd be speaking to a room full of people—not to mention national media personalities. It was entirely possible, after the coverage of his part in the incident in Iraq, that his speech could see airtime on CNN. That just boggled the mind.

Not that he cared. Honestly, he'd much prefer to be home, right now, working overtime on reminding his wife of the physical connection they shared.

She caught his eye from the first row and gave him a reassuring smile. It was brittle. To anyone else she probably simply looked preoccupied with her duties as coordinator of the ceremony. Chase knew better.

"Most of you are aware of the heroic efforts Major Charles Carden showed during his time serving the United States Air Force in Iraq. If you ask him, he'll simply tell you that on that night he was doing his job, no more. The men whose lives were saved that night would strongly disagree."

The President continued to drone on, reciting the paperwork from the medal submission and singing his praises as if he could walk on water. After several minutes he finally ended with, "It is with great honor that we present Major Charles Carden with the Distinguished Flying Cross, one of the highest honors that can be bestowed upon a pilot."

It was his cue to move forward, to receive the blue-striped ribbon and bronze-rayed cross and public congratulations from the President. He'd just stepped out for the President to pin the medal to his chest when a commotion erupted near the middle of the room.

Chase knew immediately what it was. His eyes scanned the crowd and found a knot of people surging toward a man. In the center of everything, he stood on a chair, yelling at the top of his lungs, "Don't pin that medal on his chest! He killed men and women. He didn't save them." The man brandished a black pistol.

His heart seized in his chest as the man pointed it toward the front of the stage. It wasn't directed at any one person but Sabrina was close, too close. So were his mother and sister. The President. This was much worse than anything he could have imagined. Never, in his wildest dreams, would he have thought the man could get a gun into the room. When this was over, heads were going to roll if he had to chop them off himself. Assuming he was still alive to do it...

Secret Service swooped in, surrounding the President and leading him away in a cluster of controlled chaos.

A half-dozen men from the security detail were weaving through the rows of chairs, struggling with the crowd. The scrum of media had turned, the blank eyes of their video cameras and black holes of their microphones now pointed at the shouting man instead of the dais Chase stood on.

He could see the disaster, coming almost in slow motion, just like the night it had all turned to shit. That night he'd made a decision that had cost men and women their lives. He didn't want that responsibility tonight. But the security and

Secret Service wouldn't play nice. Not with a man who'd drawn a gun in the President's presence.

"Stop!"

His voice echoed through the room, amplified by the bank of microphones a half foot away from where he stood.

Everyone startled to a stop—Blankenship, the security personnel, even several people from the television crews who had begun to race closer to the action. There was no doubt, this would show up on CNN for sure. Just what the air force needed—a PR nightmare of momentous proportions. The President had been threatened on their watch.

He needed to calm Mr. Blankenship down, at least enough to get him to release the gun.

"You don't deserve that medal!" The other man's silence didn't last long. The sound of his voice seemed to jump-start everyone else back into action.

"I know. Everyone stop!"

Chase kept his eyes trained solely on Blankenship, standing head and shoulders above everyone else. He didn't look deranged. In fact, he looked hollow, his eyes desolate and sad and…hopeless.

Security was now close enough to clear the chairs around him but didn't actually reach for him. The gun wavered at his side, erratic, with no specific target.

Chase fought the urge to search for Sabrina in the crowd, to make sure she was safe and out of harm's way. Just seeing her, the calm, collected way she handled everything, might help give him the strength he needed to navigate this situation. But he couldn't. Not without drawing unwanted attention to her.

"Why are you here, Donald? What do you want?"

"You killed my little girl." The words were punctuated by a burst of spittle, and the blank eye of the gun jerked up to meet him.

A gasp of shock rippled through the crowd, the roar of people shoving and pushing for the doors getting louder.

Chase stayed calm. He had to if he wanted to maintain control. Slowly raising his hands, he inched as far behind the podium as he could. If the gun went off he wanted as much protection as possible. He just needed to keep that gun trained on him.

"Mr. Blankenship, I think we both know that isn't true."

"I don't know anything of the sort. She died, on a mission serving her country. Because you called in the chopper to rescue the senator they didn't get there in time to save my baby girl. You lived. She died. If you hadn't been there she would have lived. You killed her."

"No. I did what needed to be done for a civilian without the training your daughter had. She was a good soldier. From a fighting family. She knew how to take care of herself. But men and women die in war. She knew that. *You* know that. She would have died no matter what that night—her injuries were just too severe."

The man's face crumpled. Chase could see what little life had been left inside him simply slipping away. He wanted to reach out to the man. But Blankenship still held the gun trained on him. Steady and true.

Within seconds the fight returned to his eyes like the ebb and flow of the ocean across sand, eating away at his stability and sanity.

"No. That isn't true. She would have made it, my baby, if they could have gotten to her. She died in the sand, in the dark, alone, cold and in pain, because they couldn't get her out."

Chase opened his mouth to calmly repeat what he'd said but before he could, Blankenship was yelling again, his face red and florid with anger and grief.

"Where's your wife?"

Chase's heart suddenly lurched against the walls of his chest. A warm gush of adrenaline entered his blood. "My wife. I don't know what you're talking about." Stall. It was the only thing he could think of while his brain raced in circles, hoping, praying someone had gotten Sabrina out of this room in the chaos.

But at the center of his being he knew his Sabrina too well for that, could feel her there, watching, waiting. She wouldn't leave him.

"Don't screw with me." The gun jerked in his hand as the older man emphasized his point with the business end of the barrel.

"I don't know where she is. But she has nothing to do with this."

Blankenship straightened, hate gleaming maniacally in his eyes, mixed with a desperation that reached through the room to the podium.

"Oh yes, she does. She covered this whole thing up. She should have done the right thing, called this farce off. Instead she did nothing. She covered up. For you.

"Where is she? Captain McAllister, I know you're here. Get up there with your husband."

Blankenship looked around the room, at those spectators and news crews that hadn't left, gathered at the edges in tight groups, hoping that there was safety and invisibility in numbers.

She shifted, in front of Chase and to his left. The smallest move from her and he'd immediately locked on. "Don't you dare, Sabrina," he said softly.

He kept his gaze trained completely on Blankenship, knowing she was close enough to hear him. But she was stubborn enough to ignore him, too.

She separated from a knot of people and walked slowly up the side stairs, onto the dais and crossed to stand next to him.

"What do you think you're doing?"

"Whatever it takes to keep him from pulling that trigger."

He grabbed her arm and pulled her behind him.

Blankenship lunged closer. From all directions, as if on command, the security who'd been circling and watching erupted. Someone, Chase couldn't see who, knocked the gun from his hand. The thing went flying, clattering to the ground and skittering to a stop at the foot of a slack-mouthed journalist.

Men in suits swarmed them both, pushing and forcing them out of the room. He reached for her, for any part of her he could touch—her hand, her shoulder, her face. But he couldn't get there. They were separated as they headed down the hallway even as he strained harder to see her. He called for her. The security force ignored him. Each step took him farther and farther away from her, more and more people crowding between them.

They bustled him into a small office where he was told to wait.

"What about Sabrina? Where's my wife?"

"We're taking care of her. She's fine."

"Wait! What?" The door slammed and he could hear several voices as men stood guard outside.

Chase jerked the door back open. He'd move every last man if he had to in order to get to her, to make sure she was safe.

Before he could start knocking heads the commander and General McAllister materialized before him.

"Major Carden, what the hell is going on?"

15

"RINA."

The voice, her father's, wasn't the one she wanted to hear right now. What she wanted was Chase. What she needed was Chase.

But even as the General walked into the vacant office they'd put her in—for her protection, they'd said—her body started to shake. It was a delayed reaction, she knew. Adrenaline and fear mixing together now that everything was okay. But she couldn't seem to control the shivers that raced up and down her spine.

The walls of her chest seemed to contract around her organs. Her lungs cried out in protest. Her heart constricted, couldn't seem to catch the right rhythm.

"I can't breathe."

Wrapping his arms tight around her, her father held her and waited for the worst of the response to subside.

"Are you okay?"

She shook her head. "Where's Chase? Is he okay? Safe?"

"He's fine. Safe. They have him guarded until they can transport Blankenship."

She nodded again, trusting her father to tell her the truth. That was one thing she could always count on. With him it was the truth or nothing, even if the truth hurt.

Then she finally pulled in a full breath of air, her first since she'd seen the gun pointed at her husband, and reality seemed to come back into focus.

Chase was fine.

But they weren't. Her mind began to whirl with the problems they both faced, the fears, the anger, the uncertainty. She didn't relish the moments ahead, but she needed to pull herself together and face them. Rina McAllister tackled problems head-on. She didn't cower in a room being coddled by her father—her father who never coddled.

Sensing her equilibrium was returning, her father let her go—slowly, reluctantly. Was it her imagination or had he held on tighter than was necessary, longer than was necessary?

Stepping back, his arms dropped to his sides. "Is it true?"

No. Still the same General, his face closed and blank.

"Yes."

And then she saw the flash of pain, of disappointment. A flash that startled her almost as much as the events that had just happened.

"You've been married eleven, twelve months and never thought to tell me?" His voice caught on the words, a hesitation that told her just how much that hurt him.

She'd never meant to do that. Never wanted to do that. Rushing to reassure him, she said, "I was taking care of it. There was no need to tell you."

"Taking care of it?"

He sank down into the chair across from her. When had she sat down?

"I've already filed for divorce. It was a mistake, a joke that went wrong."

The General shook his head and narrowed his eyes as he gazed at her silently for several moments. Assessing.

This was all going so wrong.

"I watched you tonight, Rina. That didn't look like a joke.

You risked your life to save his. You love him. I can see it when you watch him. You couldn't take your eyes from him tonight, willing him anything and everything you could give him in order to survive. Why would you want a divorce?"

Rina shook her head, tears and fear and relief clogging her throat. It was so complicated. "I don't. But we've both lied to the air force. We could lose our positions in the Thunderbirds. Chase could lose his career. It was a mistake he didn't even know about until a few weeks ago. He shouldn't have to give up everything because I made a bad situation worse. If we get divorced then maybe, maybe, he can talk the commander into overlooking the small matter of fraud. It's the only way I know to make this right."

She had to make this right. Even though she couldn't help feeling she was losing the one thing that made her right—made her whole, made her the person she was destined to be. But she loved Chase too much to do anything else. It was the only way she could protect him from the devastation of her mistake.

She looked at the General—her father—with stinging eyes. "I'm so sorry to disappoint you. I know how much my career in the air force means to you but…I think the best thing for me is to get out at the end of my assignment with the Thunderbirds. That is, if they let me stay that long."

"Oh, Rina. I don't care about your career in the air force. I won't deny that I enjoyed knowing you'd found a career you enjoyed and excelled at in the air force—it's been a good life for me and I wanted the same thing for you. But I don't care what you do as long as you're happy."

Rina stared at her father, dumbfounded. That had not been the reaction she expected. She'd expected a fight. Anger. Something. In the past few minutes her life had turned to chaos, and in the last three seconds the foundation of that life had crumbled beneath her feet.

Rina dropped her head to her hands, her eyes squinting shut behind her pressing fingers, and let her mind whirl. She didn't know which thought to settle on first. How could you choose when your entire life seemed suddenly...wrong.

She'd based her decisions about everything—her career, her marriage, her life's choices—on assumptions and beliefs that weren't true.

If she'd been wrong about this then what else had she been wrong about? Chase? What he needed and wanted? What *she* needed and wanted?

Suddenly, a weight fell from her shoulders, a burden she'd been carrying for a very long time. One she'd apparently put up there unnecessarily.

But that burden hadn't been the only thing holding her back from taking that leap of faith with her husband. She'd barely been able to articulate the truth to herself, to admit the weakness she couldn't seem to conquer. Saying it out loud, to her father, somehow made it even more real.

"It scares me so much. I grew up watching you take risks. I always resented you putting the air force first, leaving me alone at the drop of a hat because going was a good career move."

"I never left you alone, Rina."

"I know. But I didn't want nannies or babysitters. I wanted my father. I'd already lost my mother...every time you left I was so worried I'd lose you too."

"Oh, Rina, I never knew."

"I know." She hadn't told him. She hadn't wanted to disappoint him or become the miniature version of the complaining, nagging, unhappy woman who'd left them.

"I've watched him take risks." A shudder ran through her body. "I thought my heart would stop when I heard about the crash in Iraq. I'm not sure I can live with that kind of fear again. I'm afraid." She focused back on her father. "Afraid I won't be able to handle it. Afraid I'll be just like mother."

He reached across the space between them and grabbed her hands. "Baby, you're nothing like your mother."

She pulled her hands from him, standing up and whirling away. She couldn't stand the thoughts jumbled up inside her head. "I'm everything like her. Every day I look in the mirror and see her staring back. You have no idea how hard I've worked to kill the spontaneous, wild, impulsive part of her I have deep inside. And Chase…I can't seem to keep it locked away with him. With him I get married by Elvis as a joke, I smack paint on his rear and roll around on plastic."

She groaned at the back of her throat just remembering some of the carefree, idiotic things she'd done. But her father laughed, a precious sound she hadn't heard enough in her life.

Standing up from his chair, he walked to her, the laughter gone, his face sad and serious. "You enjoy life. There's nothing wrong with that. Rina, you have the best parts of your mother. Maybe I shut her out of our lives too much, took out the good memories, along with the bad ones I was trying to hide away. For that, I'm sorry."

Rina opened her mouth to say something but nothing came out so she shut it again. He stared at her. His eyes were green shot through with gold just like her own, solemn, somber and filled with love.

"She wasn't perfect. Neither am I. Neither are you. But your mother knew how to embrace life, how to find the joy in every situation. She was impulsive and fearless. Just like her little girl. If you want this, if you want him then you have to be willing to take that chance, Sabrina. The same chance your mother and I took. It didn't work for us and I can't guarantee it'll work for you, either, but I do know one thing. I wouldn't have traded the years I spent with your mother or the gift she gave me for anything in this world.

"You have the best parts of both of us. Now, all you have to do is decide what you want and use them to get it."

Moving closer, the General said, "Your commander is waiting with Chase down the hall. When you're ready the guard will take us there."

Reaching for her hand, he squeezed it tight, leaned in and left a warm kiss on her forehead. "I love you, Rina."

WHERE THE HELL was she? General McAllister had left at least twenty minutes ago to get her.

They wouldn't let him out to find her. In fact, he was under strict orders from Commander Wright not to leave the room *if he knew what was good for him.* Not even that would have kept him in this box of a room except her father had promised to bring her back. Which had been fine with the commander since he wanted to talk to them both.

But they'd been waiting in stony, tension-filled silence for so long his skull throbbed against the pressure. He'd resign right now if it would get him access to Sabrina any sooner.

He was halfway to doing just that when the door opened and Sabrina walked in followed silently by the General.

"Captain McAllister, so nice of you to join us." The sarcasm from the commander made Chase want to snarl.

"Oh, bristle down, Carden." The General's voice held a hint of amusement that he, frankly, didn't have the patience to deal with right now. Nothing about this situation was funny.

Brushing past both of the other men, Chase wrapped his fingers around Sabrina's arms and stared hard into her eyes for several moments before pulling her to him and whispering, "Are you okay?"

"I'm fine. We can talk in a few minutes, but right now I think we have some questions to answer."

"You're damn right you do. Get your hands off my public affairs officer, Major Carden." Chase reluctantly let Sabrina go. "That had better be the last display of public affection I see from either of you for the next twelve months, do I make myself clear?"

Chase narrowed his eyes when Sabrina nodded her head in a short jerky motion beside him.

She asked, "Does that mean we'll be continuing with the Thunderbirds, sir?"

"The least you both deserve is a formal letter of reprimand, especially after the damn stunt you pulled earlier this week with those notes, Major Carden. I do not take kindly to being made a fool of or being kept in the dark!"

"Sir, if it makes any difference to your decision, Chase—Major Carden knew nothing of our marriage until several weeks ago. I'm the one who kept the information from the air force. And I've recently filed for divorce so the situation should be taken care of in a matter of weeks."

"You did what?" Chase rounded on Sabrina, not caring that he'd just turned his back on a higher ranking officer in the middle of reprimanding him for conduct unbecoming.

Sabrina looked up at him in silence before staring over his shoulder at the commander.

His heart stopped beating, honest to God stalled in his chest for several moments, before his brain kick-started it back into motion. She couldn't do this. He wouldn't let her.

The commander continued talking, oblivious to the fact that Chase's world was falling apart.

"But the General has convinced me that there's no reason to ruin the careers of two such fine examples of air force ideals. However, I don't want you to think I'm happy—I'm not. And if anything like this ever happens again I'll throw the book at both of you. Do I make myself clear?"

Sabrina answered immediately, "Yes, sir." It took him considerably longer. He really didn't care about that right now. But when she looked at him, a single eyebrow raised, her lips drawn tight and her eyes narrowed in warning, he finally responded, "Yes, sir."

"Whether or not you get a divorce is completely up to you, but whatever you decide I expect the proper paperwork on my desk first thing Monday morning, understood?"

Great, so the commander didn't care. He did. He wanted Sabrina as his wife. He'd never wanted anything more. Taking a step toward her, he was intent on convincing her, with a kiss, with words, with whatever it took to get his wife back, that they belonged together. No matter what.

Before he could reach her, she pierced him with her gaze, stopping him dead in his tracks. Her mouth was straight, her face a stoic mask. She was prim, perfect, cool and collected. She was Captain Rina McAllister, public affairs officer for the Air Force Thunderbirds.

But her eyes were smiling. And for the first time since Blankenship had yelled out in the packed auditorium, the blood in his veins began to run warm again. For the first time in weeks he thought maybe this woman could really be his.

"Chase?"

This time he did reach for her, enjoying the smooth silk of her hair across his knuckles as his fingers cupped her neck.

Commander Wright cleared his throat in warning. Chase ignored him, staring straight into Sabrina's eyes. He'd break every last rule he had to in order to convince her they belonged together.

"I'll fight for you with everything I have, including the

best divorce attorney I can find. I won't let you go quietly. I love you, Sabrina Carden."

This time the smile touched her lips. Standing on tiptoe and looking over his shoulder, she answered, "I think we're going to cancel those divorce papers."

Grasping her around the waist, Chase picked her up off the floor and crushed her to him. "Tell me." He knew in his heart, but he needed to hear the words from her, see them on her lips before he kissed them away.

"Charles Edward Carden, with you, I'm willing to try anything, do anything, risk anything, be anything. I'm even willing to fly." Placing her lips to his, she whispered, "I love you."

Epilogue

SABRINA—she was finally starting to get used to it—looked down the center aisle of the MGM Grand chapel at her husband. They might be renewing their vows a few months after their one-year anniversary, but the weeks of planning and waiting had been worth it.

Chase looked amazing, just like he had on their wedding night, only this time he wore his dress uniform instead of a tux. Their family and friends filled the small chapel. Her father. His mother and sister. Jackhammer, Sadie. The officers from the squadron, including Commander Wright. They hadn't gotten to share this moment with everyone that was important in their lives the first time around. They'd wanted that chance, to say their vows before everyone, and know they really meant them this time.

The one person who wasn't here was Elvis. She'd promised Chase, although she did have a surprise for the reception that would probably make him grin that wicked, charming smile. She'd also arranged for a bottle of champagne and a single tier of wedding cake to be waiting for them in the honeymoon suite. Now *that* would make her smile.

The past few months had been hectic. Donald Blankenship was being held in a mental facility and would stand trial for threatening the President, not to mention them. Actually, there were rumors he intended to plead guilty. But no one expected he would spend time in jail. He needed help. It had taken some time for Sabrina to come to terms with that. He had threatened her husband after all, but Chase had slowly convinced her. The man wasn't a danger to anyone but himself. At least, not now.

She still had several more months with the squadron, but she'd already resigned her commission effective her last day with the Thunderbirds. It had taken her some time to decide what she wanted to do, but freelance writing had finally struck a chord. She'd always enjoyed that aspect of her career more than any other. It might take her a while to find success at it, but she was willing to put in the hard work. And it also had the added benefit of letting her stay home so they could start a family in the near future.

They'd enjoy seeing the world together over the next several months and then see what happened. Chase still had one more year after she was finished, but he was already talking about what he might do after that time. He'd mentioned flying for a commercial airline, but it didn't really matter to Rina. As long as he flew home to her, that was the important thing. If he was happy then she was, too.

She looked at her father, waiting patiently at her elbow.

"Ready?"

Before she could even take one step, he reached over and lifted the veil from her face.

"What are you doing?"

Ignoring her, he placed a kiss on her cheek, quick, no lingering here. But as he drew back, he whispered, "I'm so proud of you, Sabrina."

She'd waited her whole life to hear those words from her father. Only now, she didn't need to hear them. She already knew.

As they drew close to Chase, she looked into his eyes and smiled through the tears clogging her throat.

He mouthed, *I love you, baby,* and snarled his lip before reaching out and pulling her into his arms. His mouth touched down on hers, hot, insistent and so wonderfully familiar.

Pulling back, he stared into her eyes, his own intense with the force of his love for her.

"You aren't supposed to do that yet."

"When have we ever followed the rules?"

* * * * *

*Drag racer and construction company owner
Beau Stillwell has his hands full trying to mess up
his sister's upcoming wedding. The guy just isn't good
enough for her. But when Beau meets Natalie Bridges,
the very determined wedding planner, he realises
he needs to change gears and do something drastic.
Like drive sexy, uptight Natalie wild…*

Turn the page for a sneak preview of

Hot-Wired
by
Jennifer LaBrecque

Hot-Wired
by
Jennifer LaBrecque

BEAU STILLWELL could kiss her ass. If she could ever find him, that was.

Her temper beginning to fray at the edges, Natalie Bridges silently huffed and carefully picked her way through yet another row of big pickup trucks, trailers, motor homes and some of the loudest, gaudiest souped-up cars she'd ever had the misfortune to see. Welcome to Dahlia Speedway, where big boys and their toys hurtled down a quarter-mile track to see who could go the fastest. Quite frankly, she didn't get it.

What, or rather who, she needed to get, however, was Beauregard Stillwell. She'd called and left messages every day for two weeks with the secretary of Stillwell Construction. He'd summarily ignored them. She'd doggedly left messages on his cell and home phone. No call back.

She jumped as a car cranked next to her with a near deafening roar. Was there another wedding planner in Nashville, Tennessee, who'd go to these lengths to get the job done? Maybe, maybe not, but she was bound and determined that Caitlyn Stillwell and Cash Vickers would have the wedding of their dreams—if she could ever get Caitlyn's brother, Beau, to cooperate.

Caitlyn and Cash had the *most* romantic story. Call it fate or destiny or karma, but fresh out of college with a degree in film and video, Caitlyn had lucked into shooting a music video for rising country music star Cash Vickers at an antebellum plantation outside Nashville. In a nutshell, they'd fallen in love with each other and the place during the filming. In a wildly romantic gesture, Cash had bought the plantation, Belle Terre, for him and Caitlyn. They both had their hearts set on getting married there. However, while a faintly neglected air worked for a video for "Homesick," a song about finding where you belong and who you belonged there with, it didn't work for a wedding. Caitlyn didn't trust anyone with the renovations except her big brother, Beau.

Which was all good and fine, if Natalie could just get him to talk to her about the renovation schedule. In the two-week span of being ignored, Natalie could've lined up another builder to handle the remodel, except this was a sticking point with Caitlyn. No Beau Stillwell, no remodel. No remodel, no wedding.

And come hell or high water, in which hell might very well take the form of Beau Stillwell, Natalie was planning and executing this wedding. Cash was being touted as country music's next big thing, and being in charge of his and Caitlyn's wedding would set Natalie apart as Nashville's premier wedding planner…but only if everything went off without a hitch. She'd either be ruined or all the rage. Ruined wasn't a viable option.

Hence, she'd finished up the rehearsal dinner for tomorrow's wedding between Gina Morris and Tommy Pitchford, settled them and their families at the private banquet room at the upscale Giancarlo's Ristorante, and left her assistant, Cynthia, to deal with any residual problems. Natalie had driven the thirty miles out of Nashville and parted with twenty dollars at the gate to gain entry to the one place she knew for sure she could find Mr. Stillwell on a Friday evening—the Dahlia drag strip.

Dodging a low-slung orange car with skulls airbrushed on the front and side as it pulled down the "street" in the congested pit area, she thought better a drag strip than a strip joint. Although she had thought it was pretty interesting the one time she'd tracked down a recalcitrant groom and dragged him out of a strip club. Her seldom-seen, inner wild girl had thought she wouldn't mind doing a pole dance for someone special in a private setting.

Even though she was about five unreturned phone calls beyond annoyed, she had to admit the drag strip was an interesting place. Apparently drag racing pit areas were wherever the car's trailer was parked. She tried to ignore the stares and titters that followed her. Maybe three-inch heels and a suit weren't the dress code at the drag strip, but changing would have meant driving all the way back across Nashville when she'd had the girl genius idea of coming here to track down Beau the Bastard, as she and Cynthia had dubbed him earlier today when he'd blown off her call yet again.

She clutched her purse tighter against her side. There was almost a carnival atmosphere. An announcer "called" the race, giving statistics and tidbits about each driver over a loudspeaker. The cars themselves were beyond loud, spectators whooped and hollered, people zoomed around on four-wheelers and golf carts, and there was plenty of tailgating going on at the race trailers. It sort of reminded her of holidays at her parents' house—chaos. Although, unlike at her folks', there was at least some structure and method behind the madness here.

She passed a concession stand located behind the packed spectator bleachers and the smell of hamburgers and French fries wafting out set her mouth watering and her stomach growling, reminding her she hadn't eaten since breakfast. God, she'd kill for a greasy fry dredged in catsup right now—the ultimate comfort food. However, she was probably packing on another five pounds just from smelling them.

She walked away from the people lined up at the burger window. Directly across from the food concession, she noticed a T-shirt vendor displayed his, or her, wares. Natalie nearly laughed aloud at the one that proclaimed "Real Men Do It With 10.5 Inches."

She didn't get the inside joke and it was rude and crude, but still kind of funny. And she had to smile at the "Damn Right It's Fast, Stupid Ass" next to it.

She was so busy laughing at the T-shirts that catching her heel in a crack caught her totally unawares. Arms flailing, she pitched into a guy…carrying a hot dog and a plastic cup of beer.

"Damn, lady," he yelled, "watch where you're going." He shot her a nasty look. "And that cost me my last eight bucks."

Natalie righted herself, dug into her purse, pulled out a ten and shoved it in the man's hand. "Sorry."

Mollified by his two-dollar gain, he changed his tune. "No problem." He looked down her chest and grimaced. "Napkins are over there." He turned on his heel and returned to the concession counter.

She glanced down. Her favorite cream silk blouse with the lovely ruffle down the center clung to her in a beer bath. Bright yellow mustard and red catsup obscured the flowers on the left breast of her jacket. She wasn't sure that blouse and jacket weren't both ruined. She quelled the urge to laugh hysterically. Napkins. She needed napkins.

She started toward the round, bar-height table that held the napkins, along with the hamburger and hot dog fixings, and realized she'd wrenched the heel off her right pump when she'd stepped in the asphalt crack. She limped over to the table and grabbed a napkin.

A blonde with dark roots in jeans and a halter top

gave her a sympathetic look. "The bathroom's right around the corner."

"Thanks."

Five minutes later, she'd managed to work some of the mustard and catsup stain out of her jacket and she'd blotted at her beer-soaked blouse. She'd toyed with, and promptly dismissed, the notion that she'd be better off trading them for one of the graphic tees. No, that would make her look even more bedraggled than her stained clothing.

For the thousandth time, she silently cursed Beau Stillwell. This was all his fault. Maybe he wasn't personally responsible for the asphalt crack she'd caught her heel in, but if he'd had the common courtesy to return just one of her phone calls or, at the very least, left a message for her with his secretary, Natalie wouldn't have been reduced to chasing him all over Dahlia, Tennessee, and her heel wouldn't have gotten stuck in the damn crack in the damn first place because she wouldn't have been here.

millsandboon.co.uk Community

Join Us!

The Community is the perfect place to meet and chat to kindred spirits who love books and reading as much as you do, but it's also the place to:

- **Get the inside scoop from authors about their latest books**
- **Learn how to write a romance book with advice from our editors**
- **Help us to continue publishing the best in women's fiction**
- **Share your thoughts on the books we publish**
- **Befriend other users**

Forums: Interact with each other as well as authors, editors and a whole host of other users worldwide.

Blogs: Every registered community member has their own blog to tell the world what they're up to and what's on their mind.

Book Challenge: We're aiming to read 5,000 books and have joined forces with The Reading Agency in our inaugural Book Challenge.

Profile Page: Showcase yourself and keep a record of your recent community activity.

Social Networking: We've added buttons at the end of every post to share via digg, Facebook, Google, Yahoo, technorati and de.licio.us.

www.millsandboon.co.uk

2 FREE BOOKS
AND A SURPRISE GIFT

We would like to take this opportunity to thank you for reading this Mills & Boon® book by offering you the chance to take TWO more specially selected titles from the Blaze® series absolutely FREE! We're also making this offer to introduce you to the benefits of the Mills & Boon® Book Club™—

- **FREE home delivery**
- **FREE gifts and competitions**
- **FREE monthly Newsletter**
- **Exclusive Mills & Boon Book Club offers**
- **Books available before they're in the shops**

Accepting these FREE books and gift places you under no obligation to buy, you may cancel at any time, even after receiving your free books. Simply complete your details below and return the entire page to the address below. You don't even need a stamp!

YES Please send me 2 free Blaze books and a surprise gift. I understand that unless you hear from me, I will receive 3 superb new books every month, including a 2-in-1 book priced at £4.99 and two single books priced at £3.19 each, postage and packing free. I am under no obligation to purchase any books and may cancel my subscription at any time. The free books and gift will be mine to keep in any case.

Ms/Mrs/Miss/Mr_____ Initials _____

Surname _____

Address _____

_____ Postcode _____

E-mail _____

Send this whole page to: Mills & Boon Book Club, Free Book Offer, FREEPOST NAT 10298, Richmond, TW9 1BR